Praise for *An Unexpected Gift*

"Craver has crafted a story about motherhood and marriage that fans of Amish fiction are sure to love." ~ Laurie Stroup Smith, author of The Pocket Quilt Series

"Diane Craver writes a touching Amish romance with themes of forgiveness, hope, and new beginnings expertly woven together in a compelling story that is hard to put down." ~ Susan Lantz Simpson, *USA Today* Bestselling Author, Plain Paths Series. Southern Maryland Amish Romances Series

Other Books by Diane Craver

Amish Fiction

Dreams of Plain Daughters Series
A Joyful Break, Book One
Judith's Place, Book Two
Fleeting Hope, Book Three
A Decision of Faith, Book Four

The Bishop's Daughters Series
Amish Baby Snatched, Book One
A Plain Widow, Book Two
Priscilla's Escape, Book Three
Christmas of Hope, Book Four
Anna In Love, Book Five

Amish Short Romances
An Amish Starry Christmas Night
An Amish Starry Summer Night

Christian Romance
Marrying Mallory
When Love Happens Again

Chick-Lit Mystery
A Fiery Secret

Contemporary Romance
Because of Whitney
Never the Same
The Proposal

Historical and Christian Fiction
A Gift Forever

An Unexpected Gift

Amish Adoption Series

Book 2

DIANE CRAVER

Vinspire Publishing, LLC
www.VinspirePublishing.com

For Tom, the love of my life

Ask and it will be given to you;
seek and you will find;
knock and the door will be opened to you.
Matthew 7:7

Chapter One

"It's a beautiful night," Isabella Miller said. She loved how clear the October night sky appeared, and the cool, crisp air was refreshing. "I hope the weather will be like this for our November wedding. There shouldn't be any snow yet."

Justin Glick nodded. "It is a nice night but what makes it even more special is being with you."

She smiled at him, thinking how Justin said the sweetest things to her.

"I'm thankful we had great weather to get the crops in. Now, we can hope for a beautiful fall day for our wedding. Soon, we'll be married," Justin said.

One week ago, their bishop announced their Tuesday wedding date at the close of the Sunday service. It was called being published, and once the announcement was made by the bishop, her father invited the church members to the wedding. Although he'd seemed gruff, her *daed* had smiled at the congregation at the end of his invitation. Their Amish weddings were held on Tuesdays or Thursdays instead of a weekend. Sunday was a day when they did not work. The Swartzentruber Amish were farmers, so they kept to their tradition of having marriage celebrations after the harvest of the crops.

Since Isabella hadn't been at the church service, Abigail had told her about their father giving the wedding announcement. Isabella had been at home preparing a meal for Justin. It was a tradition for the betrothed couple not to attend the church service on the Sunday they were published. They'd enjoyed having dinner alone.

As the buggy continued on the rural road, Isabella rested her head on Justin's shoulder. "I wish with my whole heart that we were married already," she said in a breathless voice. "I know our wedding day is only two weeks away, but I'm anxious to be your *fraa.*"

Justin kissed her forehead. "I wish the same thing. I love you, but we should've waited."

"*Ya,* but we didn't." She knew instantly what he referred to because it was on their minds a lot. Being pregnant on their wedding day was not what they'd thought would happen from slipping up one night. She lifted her head, staring at his brown hair and eyes. She was blessed to be engaged to such a good-looking and kind man. She'd been in love with Justin since they were in grade school. When she'd dropped her sandwich in the dirt, he shared his lunch with her. They were among the few scholars from their Swartzentruber district. Since they didn't have a school, their bishop allowed them to attend the Old Order Amish school.

Squeezing his arm, she said, "It'll be okay. First babies usually arrive late. I remember my cousin's firstborn came a couple of weeks late. If ours is late, that will help our situation. It won't appear that I was pregnant before the wedding."

Although what they did had been wrong, it hadn't been planned. They meant to stay pure until their wedding night. It was a spur-of-the-moment situation when they found themselves in a deserted barn during a thunderstorm. They'd decided to wait for the lightning and rain to stop before continuing on their way home. When hailstones hit Justin's buggy, his horse had been skittish. Through the heavy downpour, they could barely see a barn. Once they pulled inside and were out of the storm, they felt such relief. Clutching each other tightly hadn't seemed enough. One kiss led to another, and passion took over in their young hearts.

His face tightened with tension. "I don't want to, but I suppose the right thing for us to do is to admit our sin to the bishop before we get married."

"*Nee*, I can't. Our families will be mortified that we didn't wait. I'm hoping they won't ever figure it out." Isabella was a little afraid of her father. Actually, very afraid of him. Although he was Amish and read the Bible daily, he seldom smiled and disciplined his *kinner* quickly. He believed in spanking the younger children whenever they misbehaved, and recently he'd slapped her face for rolling her eyes at him. Except she hadn't. How her sweet mother could be married to a man with such a stern personality was hard for her to imagine. Her father expected her to be the perfect daughter and set a good example for her two younger siblings.

Telling her parents that she was pregnant would cause a lot of turmoil and ruin their wedding day. Without a doubt, her father's anger would explode at her and Justin. She could see him canceling their wedding celebration and having a private ceremony. Everything was ready for their large number of guests. It'd be too embarrassing to now change to a small gathering.

Although it was customary to live with the bride's family after the wedding, she was relieved that they were going to live with Justin's family. She would miss her younger sisters, Abigail and Molly, but Justin's father needed his help on the farm. He had been diagnosed with multiple sclerosis. Between Justin and his younger brother, Silas, they had done a lot of the farm work with getting the crops harvested.

"You're right. It's better to keep quiet. And we're getting married soon. I love you."

"I love you too." Even though her mother attempted to talk her into waiting another year to get married, Isabella never wanted to wait until she turned eighteen or older. Besides, she'd be eighteen in five months. All she wanted was to be with Justin. His family never felt she was too young to get married. She studied his lean and handsome face. "We'll have a *gut* life together."

When glaring headlights flashed inside their buggy, Justin said quickly, "It seems the driver is in a rush. I'll pull over and let him pass us."

"*Ya*, because he might not see us." Her heartbeat accelerated at the thought of getting hit. Their church leaders were against adopting the orange triangular emblem and the battery-operated lights and blinkers that the Old Order Amish used on their buggies. Their Swartzentruber faith shied away from the slow-moving vehicle orange emblem because of the color and the shape. Their bishop said, "We are plain people who don't wear bright colors in our clothing."

Even though they were less willing to add safety features that might draw attention, Isabella was glad that due to the many buggy crashes, they were now allowed to put a white square surrounded by white reflective tape on the back of their buggies and could have white tubes that stuck out from the spokes of the buggy wheels. Justin had added these safety features to his buggy.

Before he had time to move over, the vehicle rammed into the back of their buggy.

Isabella screamed as the buggy flipped over and they were ejected out of their seat.

Then everything went black.

～

As she changed out of her EMT uniform, Jenna Zimmerman could not get the beautiful young Amish woman,

Isabella Miller, out of her mind. Although she was badly bruised, it appeared she had escaped any serious injury. She would spend the night in the hospital to be sure nothing had been missed. When Isabella woke up in the ambulance, she was confused about what had happened. After she remembered the accident, Isabella became concerned about her fiancé, Justin Glick. She'd murmured, "We are going to be married soon. Our parents don't know we're expecting a baby. I hope the *boppli* is okay."

Justin hadn't fared as well as Isabella. Although both had been flung from the buggy, he was the one who sustained severe injuries. When Jenna saw the mangled buggy in pieces, it was unbelievable to her that the young couple was alive. Once in the ambulance, Jenna and Amy realized they were Swartzentruber Amish. Justin had a square haircut with his hair hanging well below his ears, and Isabella wore a large bonnet with her dark dress that reached the top of her black shoes.

They were the most conservative sect of the Amish. They opposed indoor plumbing and used wood stoves for cooking and heating. Most shunned community phones, but a few Swartzentruber Amish had loosened the phone rule by allowing their members to use a neighbor's phone or have a little booth at the edge of the property. No phone number was available for Isabella's parents. They needed to be contacted soon, so she had their support during this time of tragedy.

After folding her uniform shirt and pants, Jenna put the clothing into her huge bag. She slipped on her blue dress and stuck the straight pins in the material to fasten it. She smiled, thinking how horrified her English sister Phoebe had looked when she saw her Amish sisters using pins to fasten their dresses.

She and her sister Amy were raised by Roman and Katie Yoder as their children. After eighteen-year-old Lindsay gave birth to identical triplet daughters, she tried to raise all three by herself for the first several months. It'd been too much for her, so she'd given Amy and Jenna to an Amish couple to raise. She felt it would be a stable and loving home for the two girls. Before agreeing to the adoption, Katie insisted on keeping their birth a secret and she wanted the triplets to stay together. It was hard enough to give two away, so Lindsay insisted on keeping Phoebe. Their Amish *daed* never liked keeping it a secret but he was grateful when the truth finally had come out. When Lindsay was diagnosed with lymphoma, she had to see the babies she'd given away so many years ago. She hadn't wanted Phoebe to be alone in the world if she should die from cancer. Jenna and Amy hadn't known the truth for twenty-two years. Also, their birth father hadn't known that he had three daughters.

Isabella reminded her of Lindsay. She'd seen beach photos of her birth parents when they were together one summer. It was during this time that she and her sisters were conceived. Her father, Harris Manning, had black hair and brown eyes while Lindsay had blue eyes and blonde hair. Isabella had the same dark blonde hair and blue eyes, and her facial features were similar to the young Lindsay. As Jenna smoothed her hair, she was glad it'd stayed in the bun. Now she only had to cover it with her white *kapp*. A few times she'd worn her waist-length hair pulled back loosely in a low ponytail while working instead of a tight bun.

With a loud click, she shut the locker door and grabbed her bag.

Even though Amy had already changed into her Plain clothing, she entered the locker room. "I've been looking for you. I caught Joe before he left the hospital. He said you left to change out of your uniform."

Joe Barrett had been the paramedic with them when they rushed to the buggy accident. He was English and was new to the area. Whenever there was a 911 call involving anyone from the Amish communities, he liked having them with him on the run. He knew little about their religion. At their first introduction, Joe was surprised to learn that not only were they EMTs, but also Amish. Jenna thought Joe was sweet on Amy and she seemed to like him. Their *mamm* would not like Amy ever dating Joe even though she'd never been baptized. Jenna had been disappointed that she took the kneeling vows by herself. Amy and their brother Seth planned on waiting to join their faith.

Amy wore a purple dress and her dark gray gym shoes. Although they wore black shoes to Sunday church, their district allowed wearing athletic shoes at other times. As long as they were simple and a dark color.

Jenna heard the distress in her sister's voice. "What's wrong?"

"The young man died. He had an inner cerebral bleed. They didn't get a chance to operate."

"*Ach* no, that is sad. Have they reached their families yet?"

Amy frowned, leaning against the metal locker outside the women's restroom. "*Nee*. Isabella managed to explain that their families don't have their phones to use. They use their neighbor's phone in their shanty, but her parents seldom used it. I'm sure the police or state highway patrol will go to their parents' houses to tell them what happened."

Jenna exhaled a deep breath. "Let's go see Isabella. She shouldn't be alone."

Within minutes, they were outside Isabella's hospital room. From the hallway, they heard heart-wrenching sobs. Jenna put her hand on Amy's arm, "It sounds like she knows that Justin died."

Jenna took a deep breath before entering the room. When she gazed at Isabella's red-rimmed eyes, her chest felt heavy with sadness. She walked to the closest side of her bed to stand with Amy next to her. "We wanted to see you before we go home."

"Is Justin dead? They told me he is, but please tell me he isn't." She cried out, looking confused. "I was sitting next to him. How could he die and I'm okay?" Isabella's voice was husky with unbridled emotion.

"I'm sorry Justin didn't make it." Jenna hated to confirm that she lost her fiancé.

"I'm sorry too." Amy shook her head. "I have wondered before how one passenger loses his or her life in an accident while another isn't hurt or just slightly. It doesn't make sense."

Isabella raised her head away from her pillow and took a breath. "Why would God take Justin? He should've taken me too. We are getting married in two weeks. I mean we were."

"I don't know why this had to happen." Jenna took Isabella's hand in hers, thinking how little she looked in a huge hospital gown.

"Our families don't know I'm pregnant. Justin thought we should tell the bishop, but I thought it'd be okay to keep it a secret. I'm not far along and we would have been married soon. I don't know what to do. My parents will kick me out of the house."

"They might not," Jenna said. "Will it be their first grandchild?"

Isabella nodded. "*Ya*, on both family sides. I have three siblings. One brother is older than I am. He's married but has no children yet. I have two younger sisters. We planned to live with Justin's family. His dad has multiple sclerosis, so Justin wanted to continue working on their farm. I don't know what his family will do without his help. I can't impose on them now when I am not their daughter-in-law. It would cost them more money and they have a full house. Justin has a younger brother and four sisters."

"We can help you if you're right about your family. They might surprise you though. Are you warm enough? I can get you another blanket." Amy glanced around the room.

"*Danki*. I'm warm enough. I just need Justin. I can't see living the next fifty or more years without him." She looked down and squeezed the edge of her thin blanket. "Maybe I'm being punished for what Justin and I did one time."

In a firm voice, Amy said, "It was the truck driver's fault. He rammed into your buggy. God isn't punishing you. You and your baby are alive. It is a miracle that you survived."

Jenna tucked a loose lock of hair back under her prayer covering. "It's sad that Justin died, but you'll have your baby to look forward to. That will be a part of Justin for you to have and to enjoy the rest of your life." Memories of two miscarriages entered her mind. Would she ever have a baby with Eli? *I never want to lose Eli but if I should, I won't even have a baby to love.*

"He'll always be in my heart," Isabella said, her voice cracking with sobs. After a moment, she continued, "We had supper at his house before we left for my house. We decided not to stay to play board games with his family. I wish now we had stayed longer, then we wouldn't have gotten hit by the truck. Was the driver injured?"

Jenna shook her head. "*Nee.*"

"That's *gut* he wasn't, but he'll have a hard time forgetting what happened. That will be a burden."

Jenna saw a rush of emotions cross her face and remained quiet. Maybe it was best for Isabella to absorb everything without chatter.

Isabella continued, "I'm sure I'll be sent away. My parents will be embarrassed. I doubt they'll want Justin's family to know what we did. I'll have to figure out how to support myself and the baby. I don't see how I can."

Concern clouded Amy's eyes. "It seems overwhelming now, but everything will work out for you. Don't lose your faith."

"Right now, I can't believe Justin's gone, but I'm grateful to you both. I'm glad you were on duty today. Are you twins? You look like you are."

"We are." Amy grinned. "The only difference is I'm better-looking."

"I love your black hair." She trembled slightly. "Justin's hair was dark brown. He had gorgeous brown eyes like yours."

"Was he your age?" Jenna asked, gently.

"He was nineteen. He was my future and now I need to figure out what to do with my life." Isabella cleared her throat. "It's nice you both can be EMTs and remain Amish. It surprised me because that would never be allowed by our bishop."

"It wasn't easy at first for us to convince our *mamm* to allow us to do the classes and training." Jenna turned her face away from Isabella and smiled at Amy. "She wished at first that we hadn't moved to Millersburg. *Mamm* thought if we'd stayed in Shipshewana that becoming EMTs wouldn't have occurred to us."

"I'm glad you did. It's helped to talk with you. Could you visit tomorrow before I'm discharged?"

Besides grieving for Justin, Isabella had to face her parents about her pregnancy. She had a feeling that Isabella would need another woman in her life if her mother wasn't supportive of the baby. It was difficult in their Old Order Amish district for an unwed mother, but usually, it was taken care of by getting married quickly. Now that wasn't an option for Isabella to marry the love of her life, what would she do? "I'd like to stay in touch with you," Jenna said. "I can see you tomorrow morning. If you need a ride home, Joe might be able to drive you. He has a car." She didn't mention he was the paramedic with her at the accident scene.

A sudden gasp escaped from Isabella. "*Nee*, I can't ride in his car."

"We can hire a female driver to take you home," Amy said.

"*Danki*, but unless it's an emergency, we aren't allowed to travel in a car. I don't think my parents will come this evening, but I expect they will tomorrow."

"Hi, Jenna and Amy. I need to take this young lady's vitals," Patsy said as she walked into the room. The nurse was in her mid-forties with auburn hair.

Jenna knew Isabella would be in good hands with one of the best nurses in the hospital. Patsy would give Isabella the care and compassion she needed.

"Isabella, I think Patsy is trying to tell us to move out of her way." Amy pulled on her sister's arm. "Goodbye. We'll see you soon."

"Bye, we're praying for you." Jenna hated to leave her, but she needed to get home to her husband and hug him. Life could end quickly, and she wanted to have no regrets if something tragic should happen to either of them. She loved her husband Eli and couldn't imagine life without him.

Chapter Two

"I can't imagine what Isabella has gone through. She has a long road ahead of her and needs our prayers." Jenna looked at Amy as they waited for Eli to pick them up from the hospital. They sat on an iron bench outside the building. By now their parents' general store was closed for the day; they would drop Amy off at home where she lived with Seth and their parents. Jenna wished she still lived with them. Of course, with her husband too. He got along well with her family, including her birth parents.

When she married Eli a year ago, he wanted them to live with his parents. He said it would be short-term, so she had hoped they'd find a house that was in the right price range for them. She got along fine with his father, but her mother-in-law was a difficult woman. She couldn't say too much to Eli about her unhappiness with his mother. Eli explained that some of Colleen's harsh comments came from losing his sister Sarah to the English world.

Amish parents never wanted their *kinner* to leave their faith to become English. That was what had happened to Sarah. Because she had taken her baptism vows before she left, Sarah was shunned. She could not eat with her family at their table, and they were not supposed to talk to her. The

Amish bishop approved of shunning in hopes that would encourage the disobedient church members to ask for forgiveness and return to the fold.

Amy's eyebrow rose. "It won't be easy with Isabella being pregnant. I hope she won't tell her parents until after the funeral and maybe longer. She needs time to grieve, and I'm afraid her parents will make her leave to save face in their community. I hope I'm wrong."

"If she would be English, it'd still be a big deal being pregnant and single, but not have the same consequences. English parents might be more sympathetic and supportive."

Amy shook her head. "I see what you're saying, but Mom had no one when she was pregnant with us. Her family consisted of her alcoholic and nasty mother. Isabella has family, and I'll pray that they might support her."

Jenna nodded. "It's sad Mom and Dad both tried to be together, but it didn't happen when she was pregnant with us." She thought about the details surrounding the romance between their birth parents.

During one fateful summer, while Lindsay left with her friend to work as maids at a beach hotel, she fell in love with a college graduate, Harris Manning. He'd taken the summer off before starting medical school. After he left at the end of the summer to return home to Cincinnati, Lindsay realized she was pregnant. He'd mentioned marriage to her during their summer romance. He said he'd break up with his college girlfriend. Unfortunately, Harris was pressured by his wealthy parents to marry Callie. They wanted to protect their only son from Lindsay and felt that their relationship had been a summer fling.

"I wonder if Isabella will keep her baby. She's young and probably will get married someday. I think Mom couldn't marry anyone else because of her deep love for our father."

"She also felt guilt about her brief marriage to Paul and his sudden death. He had the accident after learning she was pregnant with triplets." Jenna absentmindedly rubbed her finger over her lower lip. "It's something how years later, they finally got their happy ending."

"I'm glad we were able to be at their wedding."

"*Ya*, it was *gut* we hadn't been baptized. I doubt we could've been bridesmaids if we'd taken the kneeling vows." Amy chuckled. "And *Mamm* even attended the wedding and managed to smile a few times."

Their *mamm* had not liked many things about Lindsay and Harris. For one thing, Lindsay broke her promise of keeping the adoption a secret. Even their relatives and friends living in Shipshewana had never mentioned they were adopted. However, Jenna and Amy learned that their *Aenti* Lizzie and *Mammi* thought they should be told when they had turned eighteen.

Katie had worried about their birth parents' influence on Amy and Jenna. Then there were Harris's parents, Helen and John Manning. They enjoyed spending money on their only grandchildren, but now that Jenna had joined the church and married Eli, Katie was hopeful Amy would join soon. At age twenty-four, Amy should make the lifelong commitment to their faith.

"It's nice how our fathers like each other and *Mamm* seems happier."

"I think she's relieved that Phoebe changed her plans from becoming a doctor. Now that she's a physician assistant, *Mamm's* hoping Phoebe will meet someone and forget about Seth. I don't see her reasoning behind it, and I can't see Seth falling for someone else."

Jenna raised her eyebrows. "Seth and Phoebe seem to belong together, but it is weird when you think about it. Would he have been interested in Phoebe if she'd grown up with us?"

"*Nee*, I don't think so. She'd been his sister and when the truth came out, he wouldn't think any differently of her. He still thinks of us as his siblings."

"I suppose that's true. And we think of Seth as our *bruder*." Jenna paused, thinking how surprised Lindsay had been to learn that Katie got pregnant when they were babies. It was sad that *Mamm* hadn't been able to share her happy news with Lindsay. She easily could've included it in the letters she'd written to Lindsay. She'd been paranoid that Lindsay would want her two daughters back since Katie now had given birth to her child.

"Are you still going to see Isabella tomorrow?"

"I hope to. Did you want to go?" Jenna knew Amy had the day off too.

"I'm going to work in the store tomorrow."

Jenna exhaled a deep breath. "Seeing Justin's buggy destroyed is a reminder that we don't have a chance if we get rear-ended by a pickup truck or a car. There is absolutely nothing we can do to make our buggies safer to travel in."

"I know." Amy sighed. "I hope Dad won't learn about it."

She knew why she mentioned their birth father, Harris Manning. He worried about them traveling places in a buggy. Soon after they met their birth parents, there was an accident when they were all three in Seth's buggy. He hadn't been injured but Jenna broke her wrist while Amy suffered broken ribs. A big blessing came out of it because they went to Lindsay's house to heal from their injuries. *Mamm* hadn't been thrilled about them doing this, but they couldn't work in their store anyhow. It'd been special spending time with their newfound sister Phoebe and their real mother. Well, not real in the sense that Lindsay had been their mother to raise them.

Katie mothered them their whole childhood lives, and they only knew her as their mother. Sure, Lindsay had breastfed them for a few months before she'd given them away. Although she loved her birth parents, she would always go to her adoptive parents first for help and advice. That bond would be the strongest for her. Jenna knew her biological dad would be happy if she hadn't joined their church and embraced the English world. Jenna wondered if he still held hope for Amy. She hadn't decided what to do because she wanted to be a nurse. If she took the kneeling vows, then becoming a nurse would be out of the question.

"Or I hope Phoebe doesn't hear about the tragic accident. That might be one of the many reasons she hasn't married Seth. She thinks a buggy ride is romantic, but not for her main form of transportation."

Amy laughed. "I will never forget how Phoebe wore a blonde wig and glasses so we wouldn't notice she was identical in looks to us."

"She did a great job at fooling us. I can't believe we didn't realize she had to be related to us. Of course, Phoebe and our parents were anxious to see us and didn't want to wait until *Mamm* and *Daed* came back from their trip." Jenna grinned at Amy. "I remember how Phoebe teased Seth when she first met him in the store. He seemed flustered."

Amy shrugged. "I never would've thought he'd fall in love with our sister."

"And so quickly." Although those two as a couple seemed unlikely, they couldn't stay apart. Seth loved being Amish, but did he love Phoebe more than his faith? Jenna wondered.

"A lot of blessings came out of Mom's cancer with us learning the truth and having another sister. Of course, I love *Mamm* and *Daed* but at first, I resented not being raised by our real mother, but it is what it is. I imagine I'd be a nurse or a doctor if I hadn't been raised in an Amish home."

Jenna nudged Amy. "And we are EMTs, so we are doing something special. We are the first responders when an emergency call is made for medical help. Since Lindsay couldn't keep us, I'm glad she gave us to a stable Amish couple." Jenna hadn't liked being kept in the dark for years about their birth, but it'd been important to her Amish mother to keep the adoption a secret.

As a cool breeze brushed against her face, she thought how not having an English education hadn't bothered her like it did Amy.

"It's hard to believe that all three of us have pursued medical careers," Amy said. "When we learned Harris was a doctor, and that Phoebe wanted to go into medicine, it was a surprise. No wonder, we didn't follow the Amish woman's path to continue with the usual jobs.

Jenna's *kapp* strings bounced as she shook her head. "That's partly true except I did teach school. And look how our birth mother is a schoolteacher. I miss teaching sometimes, but I heard God's voice telling me to become an EMT."

"*Ya*, teaching is a *gut* job. And you survived teaching in a one-room classroom. I never would've made it as a teacher."

Jenna rolled her brown eyes at her sister. "I had great scholars. Well, mostly, I did."

"I worked in a fabric store which is another common thing for Amish women to do." Amy frowned. "That reminds me. Rose isn't teaching this year. Her mother-in-law thought since she married her son, it was time to quit teaching to be a full-time *fraa*."

Rose was their friend from Shipshewana. She'd taken over the teaching job when Jenna had quit to move to Millersburg. Jenna shrugged. "That happens. I struggle to live with Eli's mother as you know. Colleen said maybe I wouldn't have had two miscarriages if I hadn't been working." Sadness gripped her at the loss of their babies. It'd been four months since her last miscarriage, but she had trouble moving on and wished it hadn't happened.

"Being an EMT had nothing to do with your miscarriage. Besides, you're under the most stress when you're home with Colleen. Maybe you should let Mom and Dad help you buy a house. It'll make them feel *wunderbaar-gut*."

"It would but it might hurt Eli's pride." Jenna grinned. "I can remind him that it is a sin to be prideful." At the sight of Eli driving their buggy into the parking lot, Jenna stood. "I'll pray about having our own home, but for now, I'm *froh* to see my husband."

~

On Wednesday, Jenna went to see Isabella before she was discharged from the hospital. She met Isabella's parents while they waited for the discharge papers. After meeting them, Jenna worried about how they would take the news of Isabella's pregnancy. They seemed cautious and unfriendly around her, but maybe it was partly due to Isabella thanking Jenna for being there for her during the saddest day of her life.

When Isabella asked Jenna if she could stay in touch, Mr. Miller gave a suspicious stare at his daughter, then at her. Before she could reply, he said curtly, "That won't be necessary."

Mrs. Miller gave her a small smile. "*Danki* for taking care of our *dochder* after the accident."

If she hadn't been Amish, Jenna might understand their coolness toward her. Some Amish kept a distance around the non-Amish. Although they sent their children to an Old Order Amish school, the problem might be that she was in an unacceptable career. Swartzentruber Amish never allowed their women to work outside of their homes, so to know she worked as an EMT must have made them mistrust her. After all, she was an Amish married woman.

An hour later, Jenna was outside hanging clothes. After she arrived home from the hospital, she'd changed into an older dress and apron to do the laundry. Having the day off from work and a break from Eli's mother was just what she needed. Colleen had gone to visit a friend, so she decided to do a small load of clothes. The breeze caused the clothes to flap merrily in the sunshine.

No Colleen snapping at her for a few hours would make her morning anxiety free. In the past, Jenna had loved hanging clothes outside in the fresh air on a clothesline, but that was before she'd married and lived with Eli's parents. Colleen criticized how she cooked and even how she put clothes on the line. As she pinned Eli's shirt on the line with a wooden clothespin, Colleen's words echoed in her mind. "Jenna, you don't need to use so many clothespins."

Amy and her mother, Katie, had hung some items of clothing separately for a quicker drying time. Recalling happier times of hanging laundry outside with her sister and mother made her wish she hadn't agreed to live with Eli's parents. It wasn't just the laundry comments, but the continued criticism she received from Colleen.

Jenna's spirit became light as the breeze blew around her. She was reminded of scripture from the gospel of John that Bishop Henry used in his recent sermon: 'The wind blows wherever it pleases. You hear its sound, but you cannot tell where it comes from or where it is going. So, it is with everyone born of the Spirit.' Her faith would sustain her, and she needed to be patient.

"I'm glad you decided to wash your bloody underwear and uniforms." Colleen stood by her and pulled a shirt out of the basket.

Stunned for a moment, Jenna turned to stare at her mother-in-law. Last night, she'd rinsed her panties out as soon as she noticed the spotting. There was no reason for Colleen to be in their upstairs bathroom. "*Ya*, I started my period."

"I'm sorry." Colleen used one of Jenna's shirt clothespins to attach another shirt to it on the line.

A peaceful day was ruined by Colleen knowing about her period. It was hard enough to realize she wasn't in the family way, but it'd be nice not to have Colleen comment on seeing it for herself. "What happened to your visit with Edna? I know you were looking forward to it."

"It was supposed to be a quilting day, but we decided not to do any quilting. A few of the other women couldn't make it today, but Edna and I finished a knitting project."

At least, she didn't tell her it was a baby blanket. When she'd been pregnant before, Colleen had told her she started knitting a blanket for her first grandchild. That one had been given away to another mother in their church. "That's nice you were able to knit together."

"Edna and I had a nice chat." Colleen's eyebrows rose in her narrow face. "How is your *mamm*?"

I should tell her that Lindsay is fine and mess with her because Colleen never asks about Lindsay. It'd be nice if she did since she is my birth mother and had cancer. But that is the problem; she won't acknowledge her. She doesn't like that I was born to an English mother. "I guess you're referring to my *mamm* here in Millersburg."

Colleen threw a clothespin in the basket. "*Ya*, of course. Katie is your real mother. And a *gut* one too."

Nodding, she pinned a pair of pants to the line. "I love both my mothers and am closest to *Mamm* and *Daed*. But I love how Lindsay tried to keep us together. It must've been heartbreaking to finally decide she shouldn't raise us by herself."

Colleen frowned. "I worry that when you and Eli have your *kinner* that your English relatives will influence them too much with their wealth and worldly ways. It seems they have swayed Amy and Seth. They both should've joined our church by now."

What she said was true. Amy hadn't made plans to go to college, so it seemed it was time for her to commit to their faith. Something was holding her sister back. Why else wouldn't she take the baptism instructions? As to Seth, it wasn't his choice to wait longer but he loved Phoebe. He felt if he prayed and waited long enough Phoebe would choose to become Amish so they could marry. If Seth took the kneeling vows now, he wouldn't be able to see Phoebe and definitely couldn't marry her. Would that force Phoebe to become Amish if Seth was out of her life?

Chapter Three

Sitting next to her sweet husband on their gray sofa, Lindsay said, "I can't believe it's Thursday already."

Although she loved teaching high school math, weekends were even more special to her. She gave thanks to God daily for being married to Harris. At times, she couldn't believe they had celebrated their second wedding anniversary in June. She'd chosen that month, not because it was a popular month for brides, but because she'd finally been reunited in June with the two daughters she'd given away.

Getting Non-Hodgkin's lymphoma had been a blessing because she'd finally told Phoebe the truth about giving Amy and Jenna away to Katie and Roman to raise. Having stage four cancer forced her to break the closed adoption agreement, so Phoebe wouldn't be alone in the world. Although it was difficult, to tell the truth, Phoebe knew something had been kept a secret.

While Lindsay had been in the hospital, Phoebe had accidentally found the fourteen hidden letters that Katie Yoder had sent. When Phoebe saw the postmark on them was her birth date, she couldn't figure out why this Katie person would send letters to her mother. She didn't read the letters because felt it was her mother's secret to explain. Amy and

Jenna had been shocked to learn their two mothers had kept the adoption a secret for twenty-two years. They all had made it through this challenging time.

Harris kissed her forehead and put his finger on her chin. "We need to tell our daughters about the baby." A mischievous smile twisted the corners of his mouth as he tenderly touched her belly. "Or they might think you're gaining weight."

"Hey, are you saying I'm fat? I'm only three months pregnant and I've lost weight."

He ran his fingers through his black hair. "I was teasing you. I know you lost several pounds. I'm glad you're past the nausea now. I hated seeing you ill."

She had morning sickness for over a month and a lot of fatigue, and the fact she felt better now was a relief to her and Harris. "We can tell them at Thanksgiving. That'll be a great time." She looked forward to having Thanksgiving at their house. They'd gone to Harris's parents last year with Phoebe.

He put his arm around her shoulders. "Jenna isn't sure she can make it. She might have to work on Thanksgiving. We should tell them this weekend. I'm afraid we'll slip up and let it out in front of Phoebe. It'd be nice to tell all three at the same time."

She understood what Harris meant because it could quite easily happen that Phoebe would guess she was pregnant. It was nice having her living and working in Columbus where they lived. They saw her regularly. Although Phoebe had thought about applying for a physician assistant in Millersburg, she decided to stay in Columbus. Harris had left his practice in Cincinnati to move to Columbus. He hadn't expected Lindsay to leave her job and home when they married. Fortunately, he was able to join an established practice with other gastroenterologists.

"We see Phoebe more often, so Amy and Jenna shouldn't be jealous if she knows our news first. You're right, though. It's better to tell them all at the same time."

"Phoebe plans to go to Millersburg this weekend," Harris said. "We can take them out to dinner and tell them how they'll have a baby sister or a brother in April. It'll be a fun trip to share such a miracle with them."

She straightened and looked him in the eye. "I worry about Jenna. It might not be easy for her to hear I'm pregnant at my age when she hoped to be pregnant again. Her miscarriages were hard on her."

"I'm sorry that happened to Jenna and Eli. I was looking forward to being a grandfather, but they're young, it will still happen for them."

When Harris became quiet, Lindsay knew he remembered Callie's miscarriages. Waiting to tell his parents and their daughters hadn't just been to enjoy the special time themselves, but if the pregnancy ended in a miscarriage, it was better to wait.

Harris continued, "A lot of women have babies in their forties. They might not be surprised." He grinned. "And we're a youthful couple for our ages."

"I hope you still feel that way when our baby wakes us up each night. You might not feel so young then."

He chuckled. "I don't think any parent feels young with a newborn. From what I heard; exhaustion comes with it but also immense joy." A serious expression clouded his brown eyes. "I'm insensitive. You had it rough with triplets and no help. I don't know how you survived the first several months. I'll be here to help this time."

"It'll be wonderful to have this baby together." Tears slipped down her cheeks. "I'm sorry you missed out on so much before when I was pregnant."

He brushed her tears away, then hugged her. "It's okay. Don't cry. We're together now. It was my stupid fault."

"I get emotional a lot these days. Everything seemed to be against us." She'd forgiven his parents for telling Harris that they wouldn't pay for his medical school if he married her. In their minds, Callie was the right woman for their only child. Except she never had been, and their marriage had been rocky.

"My parents adore you."

She sniffed. "I'm grateful we're close now. It was nice your dad walked me down the aisle. That's right it should be safe to tell your parents our news." It'd been a decision they'd made together to keep the pregnancy a secret at the beginning. She was relieved to just enjoy the first trimester with Harris.

"I'll call our daughters to tell them we want to take them out to dinner in Millersburg tomorrow night."

"When we announce our news, everyone will be surprised since I had cancer and chemo treatments. And being in my forties." Jitters zoomed through her, thinking about the reactions from their triplets. How would they feel about having a sibling now when they were old enough to be mothers themselves? She hoped they would be happy for them. Leaning her head against his broad shoulder, she took a deep breath of his aftershave. The clean masculine scent was calming to her senses, which she needed. Being close to him helped too. "You smell good."

"I can wait to make the phone calls. I want to kiss my lovely wife."

She saw the heart-rending tenderness of his gaze before he kissed her. Her pulse raced at the feel of his lips on hers. She'd never tire of his kisses and to have him part of her life still seemed like a dream at times. Getting cancer had been a blessing because now she was married to Harris and a mother again to all her daughters.

⁓

On Friday evening, Eli helped Jenna out of the buggy. As he hitched their horse to a post, Jenna glanced at the restaurant. "Fancy place. Glad we clean up so well." She wore a new purple dress with a matching apron. Since it was her favorite color, she had chosen purple for her wedding dress. Many Amish brides chose blue for their dresses. Her English grandmother, Helen Manning, had been disappointed that Jenna couldn't wear a traditional white dress. Helen had raised her eyebrows when Jenna explained that white wasn't used because it wouldn't be practical. Her dress might be worn for everyday use. Jenna had gone on to say that she'd be buried in her wedding dress because that was the custom of Amish women.

When she saw Phoebe pull into a parking spot, Jenna wondered if Seth would see her sister in a white dress. Would those two be able to marry and figure out how to blend their huge differences?

Phoebe's new car was a black SUV. It looked similar to what Joe drove. She didn't need to ask Phoebe if their English grandparents bought it for her because Jenna knew the answer. Seth had mentioned when her old car needed too much work, Phoebe had given in and allowed them to buy it for her. It was a graduation present for her when she'd finished her education to be a physician assistant.

There wasn't any reason to be jealous of Phoebe about it. If she drove an automobile instead of a buggy, her English grandparents or parents would help her buy a new one. After Amy and she had finished their EMT training, they'd received a large sum of money from their English grandparents. Eli knew it would help with a down payment for a house, but he was hesitant to use Jenna's money. Amy said she'd save hers because there might be a future expense.

As her siblings joined them, Jenna thought for a moment about how crazy life could be. They were all siblings in her mind, except Phoebe and Seth were not related. Although Seth was the only biological child of their parents, she would always think of him as a brother. Life would be simpler if Lindsay had kept the secret, but it definitely wouldn't be better. Knowing her biological parents and Phoebe was a blessing. *I only wish Colleen wouldn't be concerned about my English relatives. I'm not going to leave the Amish church. It doesn't help that Amy and Seth are getting older and still haven't committed, but she should realize I plan to stay married to Eli. I'll never let go of my faith to become English.*

"I wonder what's up?" Phoebe said before entering the restaurant.

Amy frowned. "I hope it's not bad news. I wouldn't think it would be. It doesn't seem like Dad would want us to eat dinner together here if it was."

While holding the door open for Jenna and the others, Eli said, "It must be something important enough to ask us to come here on short notice."

Jenna shrugged. "We'll find out soon. I love all the fall decorations." She looked at the baskets of mums in orange, yellow, and cranberry. There were two stacks of straw with a scarecrow on each. Pumpkins were on the ground in front of the bales.

After they were greeted by the hostess, she took them to a large half-moon-shaped seating with room for all seven of them. Lindsay and Harris were seated at the end of the booth.

"This will be cozy," Phoebe said as she scooted around to sit beside her dad. Seth followed her with Jenna and Eli next, and Amy on the far end.

Jenna smiled at her parents. "So, did you miss us a lot? And decided to get us together?"

Lindsay nodded. "Yes, we have missed you. And—" When the male waiter appeared by their table, she stopped speaking.

"Hello, I'm Eric and I'll be your waiter this evening. Could I get you started with drinks?" He was a young man with reddish hair.

As they each gave their drink orders to Eric, Jenna thought it interesting how her family consisted of a mixture of clothing styles. Harris wore tan pants with a navy shirt and Lindsay wore a pretty light gray top with ruffles at the top. Her skirt was also gray. For being parents of adult children, they didn't look their age and looked youthful. Eli and Seth both wore black pants with blue shirts and suspenders as typical for Amish men. Amy and she wore their Plain dresses with their white *kapps* on their heads.

She'd noticed several customers glanced at them when they'd arrived at their spot. Were they trying to figure out how the three of them looked alike, but Phoebe wore a red sheath dress with black heels? Her red lips matched her dress, and her black hair had a lovely gloss to it. *She does look stunning. I wonder if Seth and Phoebe have plans for tonight after we finish eating.*

Harris lifted his eyes from the menu. "I hope work is going well for everyone."

Phoebe pushed a lock of hair away from her face. "Nothing too exciting. Mostly physical exams. But it was reassuring that no one had any serious health problems."

"We had a tragedy this week from an accident." Amy exhaled a deep breath. "It was a young couple with their whole future ahead of them. The fiancé died but the woman survived. Their wedding would've been in two weeks."

Ach, why did Amy have to mention the accident? Jenna shook her head slightly at her sister. *At least, she didn't mention how it was a miracle that Isabella survived the buggy accident. I don't want to worry Mom and Dad. And Phoebe. I wish buggies could be made to withstand accidents, but it isn't possible. A horse couldn't pull a heavier buggy. We have to have faith in God to protect us as we travel.*

Lindsay frowned. "That is extremely sad."

"Here are your drinks." After Eric gave them their beverages, he asked, "Are you ready to order?"

When Lindsay ordered pot roast, Phoebe said in a teasing tone, "Are you sure you want that? Maybe you should be adventuresome and try something different."

Chuckling, she said, "I am not the only one ordering the same food. Harris is getting spareribs."

"Hey, I get it—to eat what you know is *gut*." Seth took another glance at the menu. "I think I'll get the steak and shrimp."

After everyone was finished ordering, Amy said, "Now, can you tell us your news? We are all wondering why you wanted us here together tonight. And you took the time to drive almost a hundred miles to meet us. It has to be something huge."

Jenna was relieved that Amy asked because she thought their mother looked pale. Their father looked pleased so it couldn't be something bad.

Harris took his wife's hand in his. "We are pregnant."

Chapter Four

Lindsay wasn't surprised at no immediate congratulations from Jenna and Amy. Instead, she saw uncomfortable looks. Well, not from Phoebe, but she'd known her mother hadn't been ready to give up her fertility. Lindsay had decided early during her chemo that if she'd survived her cancer, giving life to a baby would be even more special. Lindsay had Lupron shots to suppress her ovaries, so she'd be in menopause during her months of treatments.

She saw Jenna's frown tug at her lips. She hadn't wanted to cause her daughter any sadness about her pregnancy, but it was a happy time for Harris and her. Lindsay hoped Jenna would get pregnant soon because that would make all the difference in their relationship. Otherwise, it would be hard to enjoy her pregnancy with Jenna wishing to have a baby too. Maybe it was too soon for Jenna to get pregnant. She wouldn't want her daughter to experience another miscarriage.

Jenna asked, "Dad, did I understand you correctly about having a baby? Or are you messing with us?"

Harris grinned at them. "I wouldn't kid about something like this. I'm serious. Our baby will have three awesome big sisters."

"I wanted to wait to tell you," Lindsay glanced at Jenna with concern in her eyes, "but since I'm past the first trimester, we decided to share our news now."

"Congratulations, Mom and Dad," Phoebe said.

"*Ya*, congratulations. The baby will be fortunate to have you both as parents." Amy gave a chagrined smile. "It'll be nice for you to raise this baby together."

Harris nodded. "It'll be great to experience everything. My biggest regret is I messed up and didn't learn that I had three beautiful daughters when you were babies. But I'm thankful to be part of your lives now."

"Did you tell Grandma and Grandpa yet?" Phoebe asked.

"We wanted to tell you, girls, first." Lindsay squeezed Harris's hand. "I hope they will be happy for us."

Phoebe laughed. "Are you kidding? They will be thrilled. Be prepared for them to spoil the new baby. Whenever you need a babysitter, I'm available."

"I don't know what to say," Jenna unrolled her napkin from the silverware. "Mom, I never thought you'd be able to get pregnant after having cancer. It's a blessing, for sure, but I have to be honest. I wish I was pregnant too." She finally smiled. "We could have fun being pregnant together."

Lindsay nodded. "It could still happen at any time. We're looking forward to being grandparents. God will bless you and Eli when the timing is right." She saw the uncertainty on Jenna's face and knew the two miscarriages caused her sadness. She hated to see her sweet daughter discouraged.

"Would you like me to make a cradle or any baby furniture for you?" Seth asked.

"That's a great idea." Amy grinned. "You might as well put Seth to use."

Relief went through Lindsay that Seth's offer made the conversation less tense. She was grateful that Amy had jumped in with something positive about her pregnancy.

Harris said, "Thanks, Seth."

"It'll be beautiful. You're talented at making so many things." Lindsay smiled at Seth. "We can talk later about the design and the type of wood to use. I won't be needing it for months yet."

Phoebe nudged Seth. "Maybe you should make more than one cradle. Mom and Dad might have twins or triplets."

"Hey, I don't look big enough to have more than one." Lindsay laughed, staring at Phoebe. "Don't scare your poor father. I'm sure we're having one baby this time."

"What are you going to do about teaching?" Jenna asked.

"The baby is due at the end of April so I'll teach as long as I can." Out of the corner of her eye, she observed Harris. She hadn't told him her plans about quitting. "I'm considering taking a year or two off from teaching. Even though I'm off during the summers, I would rather raise my child myself instead of hiring a nanny so I can continue to teach."

His brown eyes widened. "I never thought of you taking time off, but it sounds great."

After a few minutes, Eric placed their plates of food in front of each person. After he left, Amy said, "The young woman I mentioned who survived an accident is expecting a baby. She is in a bad position since her fiancé died. She's Amish and is afraid to tell her parents."

"It's sad because she should be attending her wedding and not going to a funeral." Jenna jabbed her fork into the garlic mashed potatoes. "She's only a teenager too."

"I'm sorry to hear this and she needs our prayers." Lindsay looked at Jenna and Amy. "It has to be such a shock to her. In time, the baby will give her comfort."

Amy shrugged. "She's afraid of what will happen when her parents realize she's pregnant. They're very strict and might send her away."

Sadness exploded inside her and she didn't even know the young girl, but Lindsay remembered how hard it was when she was alone and pregnant. "If there is anything I can do, let me know. I hope she's wrong and her family will lend their support. I'm afraid her parents won't want the Amish in their community to know she's pregnant though. They will feel shame that she hadn't waited until marriage."

Jenna nodded. "She has siblings, so they won't want them to know what happened. Her parents won't want the church community to know either. I feel they will have her go elsewhere to have the baby. They are a very conservative group."

~

"It's nice Phoebe is spending the weekend here. I wish we lived in our own house. I'd have her spend the night. Then I would've told Mom and Dad to spend the night too. They spent a lot of time driving back and forth from Columbus to talk with us." Seeing the house and barn ahead, Jenna wished she'd suggested a long buggy ride before going back. The crisp fall weather was perfect and there were lots of stars in the sky.

"You still can have Phoebe over." Before driving the buggy into the barn, Eli patted her leg. "And Seth can come too."

Hopefully, they'd be inviting her parents and siblings for dinner one night. It'd be uncomfortable having her English sister interrogated by Colleen. Seth was another story since he hadn't joined their Amish church. She wished Phoebe could become Amish, but at the same time, she could see why it might be too hard for her. She grew up so differently from them. The thing is Seth wanted to remain in their world and live a simple life, but one of them had to change. Did he love Phoebe enough to forget about taking the kneeling vows?

She wasn't surprised when Eli drove the buggy into the barn. Her smart husband knew she would rather walk in with him from the barn instead of being dropped off by the house. How many questions would Colleen have this time for her about their evening? She'd want to know why her birth parents drove to Millersburg just to eat dinner with them. She wanted to avoid mentioning her mom was pregnant. She still hadn't absorbed the fact that her parents could be expecting at their age when God hadn't blessed her and Eli yet.

"I think we should try to move before winter." She could even get pregnant and not have a miscarriage if they lived in their home. That might be unfair to think living with Colleen caused her to have both miscarriages, but her mother-in-law was not an easy woman to be around.

"I've been looking for a little land and a house. I keep praying we find the right spot for us to live. I want to move too." Eli grinned at her as he hopped down to take care of his horse. "You'll have to cook more when we leave. *Mamm* enjoys cooking the meals for us and it helps with you working too."

While he removed the harness, Jenna filled the bin with oats. "I'd love to cook for us, but I always get the impression your mother would rather I didn't help. She seems to like to do some things herself, especially cooking. I dream about having my kitchen. It'll be nice to be in charge." If they didn't get a house soon, she'd suggest they move to her parent's house. Her *mamm* would be thrilled to have them live there. Katie hadn't been *froh* when they moved in with Eli's parents, but their farm was closer to the hospital.

Eli led the horse into his stall. After closing the gate, he took Jenna in his arms and kissed her with ardor. His kisses made her forget about moving to another house. She loved Eli and hopefully, they'd be blessed with a baby soon.

～

While unbuckling her seat belt, Lindsay heard her ringtone. She reached inside her purse to get her phone. Glancing at her screen, she told Harris, "It's Phoebe." She laughed and asked, "Do you miss us already?"

"Funny, Mom." Phoebe cleared her throat. "Amy and I were talking, and we want to have a baby shower for you."

"That's sweet but it's not necessary. I can use your help in shopping for baby clothes and other items. That will be something for us to do together." After a few moments of chatting, Lindsay promised she'd think about a shower.

"When Phoebe gets something in her head, she doesn't give up. I don't want a baby shower." Lindsay yawned as she walked through their attached garage.

Harris opened the door to the mud room for her. "Maybe we should've had the kids come here instead. It was a long trip for you. We'll call my parents tomorrow. We don't have to drive to Cincinnati to tell them."

In the kitchen, Lindsay removed a glass from the cabinet and put it under the refrigerator water dispenser to fill it with filtered water. After taking a long drink, she set the glass on the counter. "I liked our road trip. I didn't sleep well last night wondering how our daughters would take our news. I'm glad it's done now. Although Amy loves Katie and Roman, I heard a bit of sadness in her voice that this baby will be raised by both of us."

He put his arm around her shoulders. "I'm glad we all went to the beach house for a couple of weeks."

"We should rent it again next summer."

"It was nice that we spent quality time with our daughters and son-in-law. All we can do now is to continue to spend time with each one as much as possible. We can't change the past. They know how much we love them."

She grinned. "And our daughters realize that we're deeply in love. You gave me my happy ending."

"You made my dream come true by marrying me."

Before she could say another word, he leaned over and gently pressed his lips against hers, sending the pit of her stomach into a wild swirl.

Chapter Five

Seth shook his head, holding Phoebe's hand. After they'd dropped Amy off at home, they left to find a quiet spot to discuss their change in plans. They were outside in her car near a deserted barn. "This is what we get for not telling our family about our wedding date."

She sighed. "I can't believe the baby is due in the month we planned on getting married. I'm glad we haven't told our parents and sisters that we're going to get married. We have to decide on a new date so there is no point in upsetting your family yet. It'll be hard on Katie and Roman. I hope they don't shun you."

"*Ya*, I hate to break their hearts, but I want to marry you." He kissed her cheek. "I won't be shunned since I never became baptized."

"What about your heart? Can you truly live in my world?" Phoebe asked.

Seth was quiet for a moment. He'd finally realized that no amount of prayers could convince Phoebe to become Amish for him. They'd even broken up for a few months because of their faith differences. Both had been miserable apart. "I can live in the world you and I create together as husband and wife. We'll live as Englishers, but God will be first in everything we do."

"I'm sorry I couldn't compromise and join the Mennonite church."

He'd asked Phoebe to consider joining the Mennonite church because there were many similarities to the Amish faith but differences that would make it easier on Phoebe. She could still drive her car and they would be allowed to have electricity in their house. It hadn't mattered in the long run that she hadn't wanted to because his parents wouldn't be happy for him to leave their Amish church either to become Mennonite. "It's okay. I'm happy that we'll get married in your Protestant church. I look forward to being baptized in your church. I'll invite my family, but I know they might not come for my baptism."

"Do you think they will come to our wedding?"

He shrugged. "Amy and Jenna will. I'm not sure about my parents and grandparents." He seriously doubted they would attend because to do so would appear they accepted their English marriage.

"I wish I could ask Amy and Jenna to be in our wedding."

"Since Amy isn't baptized, she could be a bridesmaid, especially if we get married before she starts her instructions."

"It was wonderful that we were all bridesmaids for Mom's wedding."

He nodded. "It was nice Jenna hadn't been baptized yet." He leaned down and kissed her. Her mouth was soft, gentle against his. Moist and warm.

"I love kissing you." Phoebe ran her fingers over his mouth. "We could move our wedding up to March."

"That sounds great to have you as my *fraa* a month earlier." He wanted to ask Harris for Phoebe's hand in marriage. He was nervous about it because Harris was a doctor. Seth only had an eighth-grade education but was studying to get his high school diploma. That was something Amy had resented about being raised in an Amish home. Scholars only finished eight years in their schools. Although their education continued as they chose their careers, Amy felt cheated that she missed going to high school and college.

Phoebe twisted her purple birthstone ring around her finger. "Are you still okay with moving to Columbus?"

"I can get a construction job there and you love your job." Phoebe was a physician assistant, but he wondered if she might go back to medical school to become a doctor eventually. Her dream had been to become a doctor, so it'd been a surprise to her parents and him that she'd changed her mind.

She squeezed his hand. "You're giving up so much for me."

"You're worth it. I have no regrets." He did worry about his parents' reaction when he told them about their wedding plans. Having their three *kinner* join the Amish church was what Katie and Roman expected of them. Once they knew their plans, he might have to move out right away. Not only would his parents feel obligated to ask him to move, but the bishop would feel the same way. He'd have to find a temporary place to live. After their marriage, they would live in Phoebe's apartment.

"I suppose we should head to your house."

He laughed. "What about our dessert? Amy told them we were getting ice cream."

"Let's pass on buying dessert. Katie most likely has pie or cake for us to eat." Phoebe grinned. "Or did you make your famous cookies?"

"*Nee*, I stopped baking after all the complaints I received from Jenna and Amy. They exaggerated and the cookies were edible."

～

Katie frowned. "What took you so long? No offense, Phoebe, but I worry when you drive your car."

"I'm sorry."

"It's not Phoebe's fault." Seth kissed his mother's cheek. "We decided not to get dessert but spent time talking about Lindsay having a baby." He wouldn't mention how the baby news had changed their wedding plans.

"That's nice Harris and Lindsay are having a baby," Katie said. "It was thoughtful of them to have everyone together to share their news."

"Do you have your delicious apple pie left?" Seth asked.

"I'll cut you both a piece." While Katie got plates out of the cabinet, she said, "Your dress is lovely. Amish women don't wear red dresses, but it looks good on you."

"Thank you."

Seth swallowed. He knew his mother wanted to know when Phoebe would start wearing Amish dresses. He wore his black pants with a blue shirt and the usual suspenders worn by Amish men. It was easier to still dress in Plain clothing since he hadn't mentioned to his parents his decision to marry Phoebe. He pulled a chair out for Phoebe before he sat beside her.

While Katie cut pieces of pie, she said, "I've tried to be patient, but I think you two need to take the baptism instructions in the spring. Amy wants to become baptized then too. That will give you time to sell your car, Phoebe. I imagine you can get a job at the hospital or one of our doctor's offices here in Millersburg."

"Where's *Daed*?" Seth asked, trying to buy some time before confessing they were never going to take instructions.

"He's in the living room reading *The Budget*." She put their pieces of pie in front of them.

"Phoebe and I want to get married in her church." There wasn't any point in dragging it out any longer. He didn't see why his *mamm* even thought there was still a chance for them to take the baptism instructions. By now, it should be obvious that wasn't going to happen.

"*Nee*, you can't. It's bad enough you've waited so long." Katie moved toward the doorway. "I'll get your father."

"Sorry. I overheard some of it," Amy said, entering the kitchen. "I'm personally glad you two are finally committing to each other and getting married."

Seth blew out a breath. "I've been walking around on eggshells. I'm surprised *Mamm* still had hopes I'd take the kneeling vows."

A short time later, Katie was back with Roman following her. In a brittle voice, Katie said, "Seth, I have prayed and prayed for you. You won't go to heaven now if you don't join our faith. You were born in an Amish family and need to think seriously about what you're doing."

At the sound of their mother's harsh voice, Amy turned to look at her. "Seth is an adult and needs to make his own decision. He hasn't been baptized so we can still be a family and do things together."

Seth was grateful that Amy spoke up for him. "I might as well tell you the rest. I'm going to get baptized soon in Phoebe's church."

Roman took Katie's hand in his. "I'm disappointed at your decision but I am not surprised."

Pushing her plate away, Phoebe looked around at each of them with concern in her brown eyes. "I'm sorry. I would become Amish if I could, but I can't. I know I'm causing problems."

Seth leaned closer to Phoebe. "It's not your fault. *Ya*, it'll be an adjustment for me, but I can handle it with you at my side."

"When are you getting married?" Amy leaned against the counter.

"We wanted to get married in April, but Lindsay's baby is due then. We talked about getting married in March instead." Seth smiled at Phoebe. "I'll move to Columbus and get a construction job there."

Katie frowned. "It seems you've planned everything out without speaking to us. Phoebe, you didn't go often to our Sunday church. You should go again. And would you consider talking with our bishop? You should both go talk to him."

Geez, his mother had to have her way. Seth shook his head. "There isn't any reason to when I know what I want the most in life and that's to marry Phoebe. I know it isn't what you wanted for me, but I feel we're on the right path with God."

Katie shook her head. "How can you say you're on the right path? You're turning your back on everything we have taught you."

~

Once inside the barn, Amy exhaled a deep breath. "I'm glad you thought to have us come here to look at your spice racks. The tension was too much in the house."

"I think I should leave tonight. I feel uncomfortable being here." Pure sympathy filled Phoebe's eyes.

Seth hugged her. "I don't want you to leave. We can go do something special tomorrow and not stay here."

"You could go see Jenna and Eli," Amy suggested, holding a spice rack. "You do such nice work."

"*Danki.*" Seth looked thoughtful. "Maybe we could meet them for lunch in Millersburg. I don't think I want to be around Eli's mother. His dad is nice, but Colleen looks at me with disapproval."

Phoebe nodded. "We should tell Jenna our wedding plans."

Amy laughed. "Not only you're my sister, but you'll be my sister-in-law too. Life is interesting."

"It was a shock when I learned I had two sisters but such a huge blessing. I feel sorry for your parents. All this has to be difficult for them." After Phoebe looked around the barn, her eyes rested on Seth. "I know you'll miss having your buggy and horse. I hope we can buy a farmhouse eventually with a barn."

Seth frowned. "It's okay. I'm going to get my driver's license before we get married. I won't need to have a horse and don't care if we have a barn."

"This barn is much smaller than the one we had in Shipshewana." Amy put the rack back on the shelf next to Seth's other creations. "We downsized on land and barn when we moved here."

Phoebe raised her eyebrows. "Since you decided to join your church, I guess you aren't going to become a nurse."

Seth knew why Phoebe asked because once Amy became a church member, she wouldn't be allowed to go to nursing school.

"I love being an EMT. I'm thankful we moved here, and the bishop allows Amish to become EMTs. I decided against going to nursing school." Amy grinned. "I have an important question to ask. What color are you going to have for your bridesmaid dresses?"

Phoebe laughed. "I'm going with red. It seems your mother likes me in my red dress. Maybe I'll wear it for my wedding dress too."

Amy shook her head. "I never heard of a bride wearing red. That would be different, but I know you're kidding."

"I don't have a color in mind yet."

"I'm going to head back to the house before *Mamm* comes out here to check on us," Amy said.

"We will too," Phoebe said. "I can't stay out here all night."

As Seth held Phoebe's hand, he wondered if he could be a *gut* English husband for Phoebe. He had a lot to do before their wedding. Getting his GED, his driver's license, and becoming Protestant were all important things he needed to do. Leaving his Amish ways might not be as easy as he tried to make it sound. Dread pooled in his stomach.

Next weekend he should talk to Harris and Lindsay about marrying Phoebe. Maybe he should move out and live with one of his construction friends. He didn't want to get his parents in trouble with their bishop and ministers for allowing him to live with them when he planned on jumping the fence to become English.

One thing he knew was that he loved Phoebe and felt God brought them together to be husband and wife.

Chapter Six

Isabella needed to share her baby news with Rebecca. She had a hard time getting away from home to visit Justin's family. It'd been a month since Justin had died.

As Rebecca poured tea for both of them, she said, "I'm glad you came. All this has been hard on Abe. And me. Justin was such a good son." She pulled out a chair to sit on. "We looked forward to you both living here. Now with him gone, we have decided to move and sell the farm."

Isabella swallowed hard. How could she look the older woman in the eye and tell her about the pregnancy? Before she thought it might bring Justin's parents comfort to know that they were going to have a grandchild. *Ach*, if only they'd been married. Things would be different. As much as she wanted to tell the truth, she couldn't bear to tarnish Justin's reputation. "I hate for you to move."

"We plan on leaving to be near Abe's elderly parents in Lancaster." Rebecca frowned. "They are in better shape than he is. It'll be nice to live there."

"I'll miss all of you so much."

"There is something you might not know. After we had Justin, the doctor told us he didn't think I could have more *kinner* so imagine our surprise when later we were blessed."

She wondered if that was why Justin had been so close to his parents. It'd been just the three of them for several years. His death caused several changes. "I feel such an emptiness. I'm not going to get married to anyone else. Justin was my true love."

Rebecca put her cup down and patted her arm. "You're too young to think this way. Justin would want you to be happy. I know it doesn't seem possible now but in time things will get better."

As she sipped her tea, Isabella knew that was not possible. Although Rebecca's kitchen was plain, it seemed cozy. "Be sure to say goodbye before you leave."

"I just thought of something. Do you remember Tom King? He wants to buy our house and land. He's around twenty years old. He went to school with you and Justin."

Why was Rebecca telling her about Tom? "I don't remember much about him."

"He isn't a member of our church district. He could be a possible husband for you in time."

"I don't want to get married. Justin was taken from me, so I'll have to be satisfied with a single life." She couldn't marry Tom, and it would be weird to live in this house, but she knew Rebecca meant well and wanted the best for her.

"*Ach*, I forgot to tell you that Abe's family isn't Swartzentruber Amish, so that will be another change."

Isabella shook her head. "I never heard this before."

"Abe left his Old Order Amish to marry me. My parents wouldn't give their blessing otherwise."

"You won't have to use a wood stove any longer."

Rebecca nodded. "His parents have a gas propane refrigerator and stove. They have indoor plumbing too. It'll be helpful for Abe to have a bathroom to use inside. That will make things easier for him."

"That will be heaven not to have to use an outhouse."

"Although there will be *wunderbaar* changes, I'd rather Justin hadn't died, and we could have our life here." She learned closer to Isabella. "And you would've been our daughter-in-law."

Tears filled her eyes. "I wish I could've been your daughter-in-law. I want to hear Justin's voice again. I miss him all the time. It's hard to believe he's gone from our lives."

"When I first wake up in the morning, I hope things will be back to the way they were. It was so unexpected to lose him. He was too young." Rebecca paused, looking heartbroken. "We can't bring him back. God had plans for Justin."

"If only the driver hadn't hit us, Justin would be here."

Rebecca nodded, "Our *kinner* miss him a lot too. Moving to Lancaster might help all of us with our grief." She let out a big sigh. Would you like more tea?"

"*Nee.* I better get home." She stood and carried her cup to the sink. "If I stay any longer, my *daed* won't be happy."

"I wish you could get out of your house."

"Me too. It's hard living with my *daed*." She rinsed her cup and dried it.

After hugging each other and saying goodbye, Isabella stepped outside. Once inside her buggy, frustration mounted within her. What would she do now? For sure and certain, it was a blessing she hadn't had any pregnancy symptoms to alert her parents about her secret. In a way, it was too bad she couldn't just marry someone and give her baby a father. That seemed as unlikely happening as the moon falling out of the sky.

She was truly alone. *I can't tell my parents the truth. I couldn't break Rebecca's heart about her son not waiting until marriage. Justin, why did you have to leave me? My love for you will never die.*

As she continued driving home, Isabella prayed aloud, "Dear Lord, please help me to make the best decision for the baby. Should I go away and give him up for adoption? Or try to raise him myself? I don't see how I can without any support, but I want to do whatever is best for the baby. I need your guidance. Thank you for your love. Forgive me for my sins. Amen."

~

"I'm going to call Mom." Jenna hadn't talked to her during the past week, so she wanted to check in with her. It was still hard to wrap her head around that her parents were expecting a baby.

Eli sat in a chair in their bedroom, looking up from his paper. "I'll miss you."

Jenna laughed, noticing how cute Eli looked. She wanted to hurry back to spend time with him. With their different EMT schedules, it was hard to be together as much as they would like. "I won't be gone that long."

He grinned. "Whenever you talk with Lindsay, you two talk for a long time."

"I promise I'll keep it short." Even though the phone shanty wasn't far from the house, she grabbed a sweater because the evening was a bit chilly.

Once she stepped inside the small building, she picked up the phone's receiver. She dialed her mother's number. Lindsay answered on the first ring. Jenna laughed. "I guess you were waiting for a call from your favorite daughter."

"Jenna, I'm glad you called. I need your help with something."

It amazed her how her mother could recognize her voice. She felt like she sounded like Amy. She doubted her mom had a favorite daughter but if she did, it'd be Phoebe. "First, how are you feeling? I've been thinking about you."

"I'm doing fine and happy you called. I would like for us to visit Isabella. She needs our support. I can pick you and Amy up this weekend to visit her. It might be nice to take her out to lunch."

"But Isabella isn't allowed to ride in a car." Jenna sat on the stool inside the phone shanty. "I could pick her up in my buggy, then meet you."

"Okay. After you contact Isabella, you can let me know if she can go. She reminds me of myself when I was pregnant with you. My mother was not supportive. Of course, maybe Isabella will be surprised by her parents when they learn her news."

Jenna exhaled a deep breath. "That will be a problem to get her to go with us. Her parents are strict, but I'll try to see if I can pick her up."

"How's work been?"

"It's been a little slow but that's *gut*. We did get a call to deliver a baby. The mother hadn't realized she was in labor at first, and her husband was out of town. She wasn't due for two weeks. She was in active labor when we arrived. I'm glad there were no complications."

"I'm glad I don't have to worry about Harris traveling."

"It's something how the baby is due at the end of April." Jenna remembered how she and her sisters were due in April but came several weeks early.

Lindsay laughed. "I was surprised to be due in April again. I remember how huge I was with you girls. I was thankful I carried you until February."

"You gave us a great start in life." Jenna glanced at the notepad by the phone, noticing Isabella's friend Hannah's phone number. She'd forgotten that Isabella might be easier to contact by calling her friend. Her family's phone was in their barn. "I'm going to get off here and try to reach Isabella."

"Thanks, Jenna."

"Get a lot of rest, Mom."

After clicking off with her mother, she called Hannah. As she waited for someone to answer or for their machine to come on if not there, she wondered if Isabella had told her friend Hannah about the baby. She was relieved to hear a young woman answering the phone. "Hi, I'm Jenna Zimmerman."

"Hello. Isabella said you might call. Did you want me to get a message to her?"

"*Ya*, that would be great. I'd like to take her out to lunch this weekend. Do you think her parents will allow it?" Jenna didn't want to mention they were not friendly at the hospital to her. They seemed mistrustful of her and Amy.

"This is strange because her parents will be out of town for several days. Her father's favorite cousin suddenly died. Isabella's family went to Indiana but left her home to take care of the livestock. Her father was not himself when he left. His cousin was the same age and it shocked Isabella's father that his cousin died suddenly from a heart attack."

"That is sad what happened. I can help Isabella with the livestock, so she can go with me to eat."

"I guess you want to talk to her about the baby. She finally told me." Hannah's voice broke. "She cried a lot and lives in fear of what her father will do. It's sad that his cousin died but I'm glad her parents and siblings are away."

Jenna ended the conversation by giving her phone number. She wanted to make sure Hannah had it too.

Should she call her mom back? *Nee*, she didn't know if they were going for sure this weekend. She'd call her later when she had more information. Right now, she wanted to hurry back to the house to see her good-looking husband.

Jenna laughed when she saw him eating a piece of pie at the kitchen table. "You have pie already."

"*Ach*, you caught me." He grinned. "Sit and we can share it."

"Colleen makes *appeditlich* pies," she said, after swallowing a forkful of apple pie. She loved his dark blond hair with a bit of wave to it. "Where are your parents?"

"They went to see Sarah. I have to say they never give up on trying to get her back in our community. They took her food. *Mamm* said she missed her and couldn't wait to see her. Sarah was always close to *Daed*, so he was anxious to go too."

"Shunning is hard on everyone." Jenna wiped her mouth with a napkin. "I've had two recent shocks. I still can't believe at times that Mom is pregnant, and Seth is going to become English and marry Phoebe. Seth loved growing up Amish."

Eli smiled. "How about another shock?"

"Is it a *gut* one?"

He nodded. "I found a beautiful house for us to buy. It has a small barn and fifteen acres."

Jenna gave Eli a big kiss on his lips. "Is it empty so we can move in before winter?"

"*Ya*, it is. We can look at it tomorrow after work, then go out for supper."

"You're the best husband ever." As soon as he finished eating the pie, she would hurry to clean up the pie plate and show him in their bedroom how special he was to her.

"I wish I'd found a house earlier. You are so *froh* and grinning at me all the time."

"I doubt I can sleep tonight. I'm so excited."

Chapter Seven

Jenna liked listening to the realtor, Cathy Hutton, talk about the house they were looking at because she hoped they could buy it. The realtor looked thin in her black pants and turquoise blouse. It was great that Cathy could answer all their questions. It was nice to have someone so knowledgeable. Jenna continued to listen to the realtor's pleasant voice as she pointed to the lights in the rooms.

"I love how they have battery-powered lights hanging from ceiling hooks. I noticed not all Amish homes have this type." Cathy smiled at both of them.

Eli nodded. "That's true. I'm glad they have these lights. The propane gas lights make the house hot in the summer. Or kerosene lamps are used by some, but they don't put out much light."

"All Amish districts have different rules. Some are more conservative and don't allow plumbing in the houses. We are all the same when it comes to not having electricity in our homes." Isabella came to Jenna's mind, realizing she'd see her house tomorrow when she picked her up for lunch. It was doubtful there would be anything in her Amish Swartzentruber house like this beautiful home with many wonderful details.

Eli took her hand as they walked to look at the first-floor master bedroom. "I like the oak hardwood floors are the same as the kitchen and living room floors."

"The blue walls are pretty and a nice change from the beige walls in the other rooms." Jenna took a deep breath. Would they be able to buy this house? So far, she loved everything she'd seen in it.

"What do you think of the size of the bedroom?" Cathy asked, glancing at her real estate paper. "It says it is 14 x 16 so there should be plenty of room for your bedroom furniture."

As Eli looked at the area, he said, "Our armoire is a pretty big one, but there definitely is room for it."

"Our dresser is huge too." Amish homes didn't have closets, but they didn't have a lot of clothes. *Phoebe could never fit all her English clothes in an armoire,* Jenna thought. "I like they have a small battery-powered lamp on a stand next to the bed. It might not be enough light to read by but will help me to see if I have to get up in the night to use the bathroom."

"Jenna, I'm glad you mentioned the bathroom. There is one in the hallway right outside the bedroom."

If she ever got pregnant, it'd be great to have a bathroom close to the bedroom. If only she was pregnant now, life would be perfect, Jenna thought. "The builders thought of many features for this house."

As Cathy led them to the bathroom, she continued, "I have to admit I was surprised at how the bathrooms look like mine with showers, tubs, and sinks."

"Some Amish use outhouses instead of having bathrooms because they feel having bathrooms are too worldly. They want to live plainer than some of us do," Eli explained. "We're Old Order Amish, so we have indoor plumbing."

"I didn't know that." She glanced at her paper. "There is natural lighting in the bathroom upstairs. They have a skylight according to my listing. This is the first time I've shown this house. I have another Amish couple scheduled to see it tomorrow."

"That surprises me. I figured you had shown it already. You've been wonderful at answering our questions," Jenna said, twisting her *kapp* tie around her finger. "Don't do too great of a job for the next couple."

Eli shook his head. "I guess you must want this house."

Jenna grinned. "*Ya*, I do."

After seeing the four bedrooms upstairs, Jenna wondered if she and Eli would have *kinner* to fill the rooms.

Forty minutes later, they were seated at a corner table in an Italian restaurant. With candles flickering against the crisp white tablecloth, Jenna loved the romantic atmosphere. "*Danki* for bringing me here. It's wonderful."

"I heard another EMT talk about how much they enjoyed eating here."

Jenna waved her garlic breadstick at Eli. "I love there is a good-sized basement where we can hold our church meetings. I can't believe there was a standard washing machine in the basement like the English have. I expected to see the wringer type like our parents have."

"It was something how it's powered by a diesel engine." Eli sipped his coffee. "I heard a lot of the Amish in Lancaster have the English conventional washing machines and are like the one we saw."

"*Danki* for taking me to this house. I love it. I hope we hear good news about our offer."

"We wrote the contract for the asking amount of $280,000. We should get the house. I thought about offering less but the price is right for it." He chuckled. "It was hard to offer less when you kept saying how much you loved the house."

"I'm glad because the other couple might want to buy it. I hope they don't offer more for it." Jenna took a bite of her salad. "Everything is *appeditlich*."

"It's good the owners aren't taking the appliances with them, but we will need furniture for every room. If our parents and grandparents want to give us any pieces of furniture, that'll be great."

She smiled over her plate of lasagna. "We don't need anything for our bedroom. It was sweet of Seth to make our furniture for a wedding gift. And Phoebe and Amy paid for the wood."

The waitress appeared by their table and put down another basket of breadsticks. After picking up their empty basket, she asked, "Would you like more coffee?"

"*Ya*, please," Jenna said. "Thank you for the breadsticks."

"You're welcome. I'll be right back with a fresh pot."

"Geez, we didn't even ask for more breadsticks." Then Jenna realized Eli hadn't responded to the waitress at all. "Are you all right?" she asked, looking at him.

"It just hit me how much we will be in debt for this house."

She reached across the table and picked up his hand. "It's not only a house we're buying but a farm. We won't have to build a barn. And it is a perfect size for our buggies and horses. We have land to have a big vegetable garden and to raise a crop. We have two incomes and there is the money we haven't spent from my English grandparents. We should use some of it now to pay off some of the house if they accept our offer. I'm glad you were more patient than me and waited to find the right house for us. God has blessed us."

"I still have the wedding money that my parents gave us as a gift. We can use that to make payments ahead and get the mortgage paid off faster."

"What did your parents say about us looking at the house?" Colleen and Jim had left before they arrived home to change their clothes for their house tour.

"I talked to them yesterday, so they'd know that we wouldn't be home for supper." Eli shrugged. "*Daed* seemed pleased we found something to look at and that it isn't far from the hospital. *Mamm* said she was glad we had lived here after our wedding." He smiled. "She was happy to have her son home a little longer."

Jenna couldn't help herself and rolled her eyes. Colleen's favorite child was definitely Eli and if they lived at their house forever, she'd be in heaven. "Your mother had you at home long enough. It's my turn to have you to myself."

"What can I say? I must be adorable with you two so in love with me."

She raised her eyebrows. "And conceited."

～

On Saturday, Jenna pulled into Isabella's dirt driveway. Seeing the small farmhouse surprised her because she knew Isabella had three siblings. It must have been crowded before her brother had moved out of the house to get married. As she glanced at the Miller's house, Jenna noticed it needed to be painted. It looked like it had once been white but now the wood looked gray and weathered. She felt thankful that Lindsay had given her to Katie and Roman. She had received love, and support, and never lacked for anything. Lindsay had chosen an Amish family wisely in her opinion.

When they first learned they had been adopted, Amy resented not being the one chosen by Lindsay to raise. She thought going to an English school where they taught science would have been better. Amy said she might have gone on to medical school and become a doctor. Jenna loved her biological parents, but she couldn't imagine being raised by them. If she had been, Eli might not be her husband now. She loved being married to him and her heart broke that Isabella had lost her fiancé.

Isabella had a decision to make about her baby. Maybe she should encourage her to put the baby up for adoption if her parents wouldn't support her in raising their grandchild. That might not be for the best. What if she gave the baby up only to regret it later?

"Hello. *Danki* for coming here." Isabella climbed into the buggy quickly. She wore a black dress which was longer than the dresses Jenna wore.

"How's it going with keeping up with the farm chores?"

"I gathered the eggs before you came and fed the chickens. My *daed* asked Aaron, a neighbor, to help me with milking our cows. We did that early this morning and of course, will again later today."

Jenna concentrated on missing the ruts as she turned Homer to go back on the road. She didn't want the horse to get hurt.

Pointing to small stones along the side of the driveway, Isabella said, "Justin placed the stones there to shelter the driveway from heavy winds and break up any water that might flow across the driveway. He liked to do things for my family."

"He sounds like a *wunderbaar* man." Jenna turned to look at her friend. "Are you feeling okay?"

"*Ya*, I haven't had any nausea. That helps to keep my pregnancy a secret from my family." Isabella frowned. "I wanted to share the news with Justin's mother, but I couldn't do it. She mentioned how he was the perfect son. Also, they are selling their house soon and moving to Pennsylvania."

"You should still tell her about the baby. It might bring her comfort that a part of Justin will live on. And she could be a source of comfort for you. Maybe you could even move with them."

She shook her head. "His parents would be crushed that we didn't wait until marriage."

Jenna figured she was embarrassed, to tell the truth. "At first, they might be shocked, but later it might be a blessing to them to have a grandchild. I'm sure you aren't the first in your church community to be pregnant and to get married later. Just pray about it and maybe you'll change your mind about telling them. I'm glad you told your friend, Hannah. You need to have support during this time and someone to talk to. If you ever need to talk to me, don't hesitate to call me."

"*Danki*, I will." Isabella gave her a small smile. "Just be careful when leaving a message. I'm happy to get out of the house today, but it'll be another secret from my family." She sighed. "I wish I could be honest. My parents are not the understanding kind. I'm surprised they left me to stay at home alone, but they said Hannah could visit me."

"Has she visited you?"

Isabella nodded. "We had supper together yesterday. I was glad she could get away for a few hours."

"That's *gut* you have a close friend. We're meeting my mother at a cute place called The Red Mug Coffee Company. Amy has to work today because another EMT called in sick. She's sorry to miss you."

"That's disappointing. Tell her hello for me."

Fortunately, there was little traffic traveling to Millersburg. When Jenna pulled the buggy into a spot next to a hitching post, she hoped her mother had saved them a table. The coffee shop wasn't big but popular with being right in the center of Amish country.

After Jenna hitched Homer to the post, they entered the cafe. Instantly, Jenna saw her mom waving to them from her table by a window. She imagined her mother had arrived early to be sure to get a table for them. Once they stood by her, she said, "Hi, Mom. This is Isabella."

As they took their seats, Lindsay smiled at Isabella. "It's nice to meet you. I'm happy you were able to come. This is my first time here, but I love it already. I got this delicious pumpkin spice latte while I waited for you."

Jenna laughed as she sat next to her mom. "Isabella, she loves anything pumpkin, especially ice cream." She noticed there were several Amish and Mennonite customers at tables. "It's a cozy place. Did you see the menu?"

Lindsay nodded, handing her a menu. "I'm going to get the chicken salad served on a croissant with the greens."

"That sounds *gut.* I'll get that too. This is such a treat to have a meal away from home. *Danki* for inviting me."

"I'll get the ham and cheese sandwich." Jenna grinned. "Eli and I went out last night to eat, so I'll get spoiled eating out twice."

Lindsay ran her finger over the rim of her cup. "Isabella, I was like you at one time. I think you know that I was too young to raise my babies. My mother wouldn't give me any support at all. I had no other family. I hated I couldn't keep all three but felt Katie and Roman would be wonderful parents for Jenna and Amy. I knew they would be surrounded by love." She squeezed Jenna's hand. "I was right. My beautiful daughters grew up in a good, loving, and stable home. If you ever need anything or just want to talk to me, please feel free to call me. I experienced a loss except their father hadn't died. He was engaged to someone else. I'm so sorry you lost Justin."

"It still seems unreal to me that he's gone." Isabella exhaled a deep breath. "I don't know what to do about our baby. I'm hoping my parents will surprise me, but they probably will send me away out of embarrassment. I don't know where though. I don't have grandparents. My *daed's mammi* died from pneumonia and his *daed* had a stroke. My *mamm's* parents died in a house fire."

Lindsay said, "That's too bad you don't have any grandparents."

"I can see why you couldn't raise triplets. It's sweet you kept one daughter. I don't know if I can raise one baby."

"You don't have to decide now," Jenna said.

An attractive Amish waitress appeared by them, smiling at Lindsay. "I see you aren't by yourself any longer. I can take your orders if you're ready."

After they gave their orders, Isabella glanced at the waitress as she walked away. "I could never work anywhere. In our community, Amish women don't get jobs and stay at home. It'd be nice to have a job and make my own money."

Lindsay looked thoughtful. "Would you be allowed to do some sewing at home to make extra money? I could use a few maternity clothes."

Her blue eyes widened. "I didn't know you were pregnant. Congratulations."

"*Ya*, I'll be a big sister at my age." After the waitress handed a cup of coffee to Jenna, she continued, "I'm hoping I'll get pregnant soon so we can have them play together someday. I've had two miscarriages."

Isabella stared at her cup of tea. "Life is strange. I'm single and pregnant and you're happily married and want to get pregnant. I hope it happens for you soon. You'll be a great mother."

"I pray you'll get pregnant." Lindsay patted Jenna's arm. "If you get the house you want, it might happen after you get settled." Turning to Isabella, she smiled. "Now when I pray for you, I can picture you in my mind. You'll have a beautiful baby."

Chapter Eight

At the end of the day, Seth put his tools away and got ready to catch his ride back home. He was grateful that he hadn't been asked to move out of his home. Or rather his parents' house. Seth knew the bishop and his parents hoped with him living at home, there would be more time to convince him to not leave their faith. That wouldn't happen.

Sure, the ideal situation would be if Phoebe could join the Amish church, but she didn't want to leave her Protestant faith and her world. He came to respect her feelings and realized he could make changes for the woman he loved. Next year, he'd be married to Phoebe and living in Columbus in her apartment. As he climbed in the van for the trip home, he wished she'd consider moving to Millersburg. He liked his construction job and knew he'd miss the guys he'd worked with for the past several years.

He couldn't see her agreeing to move from Columbus with her mother's baby due in April. She and Lindsay had such a close mother-daughter relationship. It'd been only the two of them for years until Harris had learned about his triplets. A thought occurred to him how Harris had left his thriving medical practice in Cincinnati to move to live in Columbus. Here, he was doing the same thing moving from his job to make Phoebe happy. Of course, he wasn't leaving a doctor's practice as Harris did. *If his future father-in-law could adjust and work with new doctors, I should be able to find a job and make new friends.*

Phoebe, Lindsay, and Haley were shopping for her wedding dress today. Lindsay's wedding dress she wore when she'd married Harris was too short for Phoebe to wear. Haley would be Phoebe's matron of honor, but he hadn't chosen the best man. His friends were Amish so they wouldn't be able to be in the wedding. It was a shame that Amy and Jenna couldn't be attendants. They were in Lindsay's wedding but hadn't started their baptism instructions. Amy planned on starting the classes in the spring. If their bishop gave his permission, maybe Amy could be an attendant with the wedding being in March.

"Hey, Seth. We'll be at your house soon." The driver glanced in his mirror to look at him. "You've been quiet today."

Seth stared at the driver, Dan. He'd started driving the van when he'd retired from his teaching job. He didn't look old enough to retire with his brown hair and a few wrinkles on his face. "*Ya*, I have a lot on my mind but it's all good."

Once the van made the last stop at his house, Seth said goodbye to Dan.

"See you on Monday. Have a good weekend, Seth."

"You too," Seth said. Seeing Veronica's buggy as he walked toward the house, he groaned. Did his *mamm* invite Veronica? Why couldn't she accept he was going to marry Phoebe? Maybe it wasn't Veronica, but her mother visiting. He hoped to sneak in without seeing anyone, so he decided to go to the front door instead of the back door by the kitchen.

"Is that you, Seth? Guess who is here? She brought a chocolate cake for us."

As he shut the door, Seth cringed at the sound of his mother's voice. It was Veronica. Why would she bring a dessert for him when he'd never shown her any interest? She had to know he was engaged to Phoebe. Some ministers in their district were unhappy about his living at home while making plans to leave their faith. The Amish grapevine was in full mode about him and Phoebe. Was Veronica delusional about his love for Phoebe? Besides, she had joined their church and had taken the kneeling vows a couple of years ago. She shouldn't be hanging around him.

Entering the kitchen, he tried to smile at Veronica and his *mamm*. "Hi. I'll be back after I take a shower."

Veronica gave him a disappointed look. "I already cut you a big piece of cake. Why don't you eat it *first*, then take your shower?"

When his mother opened her mouth to argue, he held up his hand. "I'm dirty. I'll be quick."

Seth took his time, hoping Veronica would take the hint and leave. After getting out of the shower and drying off, he looked at his cell phone. Although cell phones were off-limits for Amish families, the bishop had given Seth permission to have one for his construction job. His boss hadn't liked to leave messages on their answering machine in their barn. He saw a text from Phoebe. He read that she'd found the perfect wedding dress. *We can get married this month then since you have your dress,* he texted back. When she didn't reply, Seth decided to see if Veronica had left.

His jaw dropped at the sight of her still at the table with the cake in front of her. No one else was in the kitchen. Strange, his mother wasn't cooking supper. "Sorry, it took me longer. I wanted to check my texts from my fiancée. Phoebe found her wedding dress today."

"You shouldn't marry Phoebe. You'll regret it when you realize how you have given up everything for an Englisher. Not only that but Phoebe is an identical sister to Amy and Jenna. Don't you find it weird to marry Phoebe when she looks like your sisters? How will you explain it to people when they see all three together and learn they are identical triplets and two are your sisters? It's disgusting to me, and it should be to you."

"You forget that she wasn't raised in my family, so I have no brother-sister bond with Phoebe. From the beginning, I never saw any resemblance between her and my sisters. Although she has black hair and brown eyes like Amy and Jenna, that is the only similarity. Her personality is completely different. We have chemistry between us and sure, we broke up because of our faith differences but we couldn't stay apart."

"I don't buy it when they are identical but apparently, it works for you."

"Veronica, I don't want to hurt you but we were never a couple. Why don't you find someone who will make you happy?"

She fingered the edge of the white tablecloth. "I've wanted to be your *fraa* for a long time. You are everything I want in an Amish man."

"I'm not going to be Amish much longer. It'd be best if you didn't come here anymore. I love Phoebe and we're getting married in March."

"Your *mamm* said I still had a chance. She never mentioned you had a wedding date." Veronica stood, grabbing her cake. "I thought there were times when you liked me. When you made the birdhouse for my brother, you seemed happy to see me. You took me for a buggy ride, and I thought that meant something."

"You asked me to take you home," he said in a soft voice. "I'm sorry. I can see that my mother caused some of this confusion on your part. I never meant to give you false hope. I'll pray for you to meet someone to love. You deserve to be happy with the right Amish man."

After lifting the cake by the container handle, Veronica said, "You don't have to pray for me to find an *ehemann*. There are several men I can date. I was foolish to wait on a loser like you."

⁓

"I want to move but where can I go for a few months until our wedding?" The whole interference with his mother and Veronica had been the last straw. He loved his *mamm* but her constant meddling was too much to handle. Talking with Phoebe would calm him down, but he wished it would be in person instead of on the phone.

"The only place I can think of is Jenna and Eli's house," Phoebe said. "You could pay them rent and that would help them with their house payments."

"I thought of them but I don't know. This is their first house and I hate to ask. Jenna seems pretty excited to have her own house with Eli."

"I can tell from your voice that something happened, and it must be why you want to move so close to our wedding. You can tell me."

He exhaled a deep breath. "When I came home, Veronica was here. *Mamm* made her think she still had a chance with me. Can you believe that?"

"I don't understand. I never thought an Amish woman would throw herself at an engaged man."

In a firm voice, he said, "It won't happen again. I made sure Veronica understood that there had never been any-thing between us and never will be."

"Our wedding is only four months away. You'll be com-ing to Columbus in a few weekends. That will give you a break from Katie. I know it's hard on her to lose you to my world. How is Roman treating you?"

"He's fine around me." He laughed. "In fact, I'd say that you have won him over."

"I can't imagine that." Phoebe cleared her throat. "I feel terrible that I can't change for you. I've made your life so complicated. It is crazy that you're the biological son and leaving when my adopted sisters want to remain Amish. I get it that Amish parents think there is no pain worse than a child who refuses to join their church."

"I have no regrets. I love you, Phoebe. Becoming English for me is easier than you switching to Amish. I feel it is what God wants me to do." He paused for a moment, then asked, "I got your text about your wedding dress."

"I love it and I don't think it will need any alternations. If I gain weight before March, then it will." She giggled. "I have more news and hope it'll be okay with you. Mom and Dad are paying for us to go to Hawaii for our honeymoon. It's their wedding gift to us. We can take the cruise tour or fly to Maui."

He was speechless for a few seconds because he'd thought about renting a cabin in Gatlinburg for their honeymoon. "I planned on arranging our honeymoon trip, but it wasn't going to be Hawaii. That's out of my pay range."

"We don't have to accept their present. I'll tell them to hold off on making the arrangements."

"I feel bad if we turn it down, but we can talk about it more when we see each other. Amish aren't allowed to fly but I won't have to worry about that. I haven't traveled on a cruise ship either." Going to Hawaii seemed extravagant to him, so he needed time to wrap his head around such a trip.

"We can think about it. I'm excited because I have never gone to Hawaii. We can both enjoy it for the first time together, but I like you planning our honeymoon for us too."

"Maybe we could go for our first anniversary to Hawaii."

"We can do that. I wish we were seeing each other this weekend. I miss you. I could visit you on Sunday for the day."

"That's four hours of driving for one day but I do miss you too. I'm sorry I had to work today." When his boss asked him to work on Saturday, he couldn't turn down the extra hours.

"I hate to miss going to church with you, though."

"We don't have church tomorrow." He thought it nice how Phoebe's church was every Sunday. The Amish didn't have a church building, so they met every other week at someone's house or barn. On the other Sundays, scripture reading was done in the home by the head of the house usually. As he heard the hesitation in Phoebe's voice, Seth said, "We'll see each other soon on Thanksgiving. I'm excited to be with your family."

After they chatted for a few more minutes, Seth left his bedroom to go downstairs. He saw Amy carrying two pizzas. "Now I see why *Mamm* isn't cooking supper."

"I'm sorry I'm running late." Amy placed the pizza boxes on the kitchen counter. "Let's use paper plates tonight."

From the living room, his parents came into the kitchen. "The pizza smells *wunderbaar.*"

Amy frowned. "Oh no, Seth. I forgot you don't like pineapple on your pizza, but it's only on one."

"That's okay. I can eat a couple of pieces from the one *without* the yucky pineapple." He knew she was teasing him about the pineapple.

"I can't fool you." Amy grinned at him. "There is only pepperoni and bacon on one and the other one has mushrooms with the pepperoni."

After they had pizza on their plates and iced tea drinks, they bowed their heads to pray silently. When Roman cleared his throat, they raised their heads. "*Danki* for getting the pizza."

"You're welcome." Amy picked up her slice of pizza. "It's nice to have a pizza night."

Within a few minutes, Amy asked Seth, "Are you feeling okay? You're quieter than usual."

"Today was a surprise for me, but it's fine now. I got things straightened out."

"Veronica came in the store today." Katie gave an apologetic glance at Seth. "She asked about you. I'm sorry I interfered."

"It got me thinking I shouldn't still be living at home when I'm not going to take the instructions. I don't know where to live for a few months." Since Veronica's visit, he hadn't felt right about living at home. He couldn't stop thinking about how much he wanted to move elsewhere.

"What does the future Mrs. Yoder say about you moving?" Amy asked.

He shrugged. "She said I'll be going to Columbus for a few weekends. And it's not long until we'll be married."

Amy wiped her mouth with a napkin. "This pizza tastes so good. I can't believe my little brother will be married before me."

"You should get our matchmaker mother busy on finding you a spouse." *That will be perfect and keep his mother from trying to run his life*, Seth thought.

"Amy, you should go to the youth activities," Katie suggested.

She raised her eyebrows. "*Mamm*, I'm too old to attend them which seems like I've mentioned before. Jenna and Eli had me over to play board games and invited Noah Hilty from our church district. I'm not sure why they thought he could be someone for me. He's younger than I am. I'm sure he's in the age group that attends the youth get-togethers."

"Noah's a nice man and it doesn't matter if he's a few years younger than you."

"There is someone interested in me. He's an EMT and his name is Joe Barrett. Unfortunately, he's English so don't worry I won't date him."

Katie tapped her fingers on the table. "I hope not. One child leaving to marry an Englisher is enough."

Seth kept quiet about his mother's comment and hoped someday she'd accept his decision. In the meantime, he would look for another place to live.

Chapter Nine

Isabella's throat closed with grief. Big sobs broke from her body as she stood in the neighbor's shanty. It was the only place she could work through her immense sorrow at losing Justin. It wouldn't do for her siblings or her parents to hear her. And they would in their small house. Sure, she'd cried at the funeral, but now she couldn't stop the abundance of tears. Overwhelming grief sucked the life out of her.

For weeks, she'd told herself that Justin wouldn't want her to break down, but she couldn't hold it in any longer. She longed to see his handsome face again.

They were in love and happy about their future together. How could Justin's life be taken so quickly? If they hadn't gone for a buggy ride that evening, Justin would still be alive. She had no hope and no future. Although she had a baby to love, how would she raise a child by herself?

She should've told Justin's parents about the baby, but it was something you said in person. They'd left Millersburg last week and were starting their new life in Lancaster. When she'd gone to say goodbye, she wanted to tell them about their grandchild. There was a lot of commotion in their house. Neighbors were there to help load their boxes in a U-Haul, so she hadn't a chance to make her important baby announcement. She'd been surprised to see Tom King there too. He'd bought the Glicks' house and it made her sad. Abe and Rebecca had been an important part of her life. With them living several hours away, she knew her connection with them had ended.

Thanksgiving would be in a few days but what did she have to be thankful for? Maybe that her family hadn't suspected her pregnancy. She'd been extremely tired but had no nausea or vomiting. Jenna wanted to take her to see an obstetrician sometime. She said it'd be fun for her to hear the little one's heartbeat.

I definitely can't see our Amish midwife. My family won't want this piece of news to spread in our community. Maybe I should just tell my parents after Thanksgiving that I'm pregnant. Get it out in the open and deal with their anger. If I wait, it could be worse. No, I can't tell them yet. Their reactions could be frightening. They will take me to Indiana to live with a relative. I don't want to live in Indiana.

If I had money, I could get on a bus and go somewhere to live. There isn't any reason for me to stay here. I can leave a letter saying it is too hard to stay here without Justin. I can put the baby up for adoption, then return home. No one has to know about the baby.

A sweet memory of last year's Thanksgiving crossed her mind. After eating dinner with her family, Justin and she played board games with her siblings. Then she'd left with Justin to go to his family's house for dessert. She'd snuggled against him when they were in his buggy under the stars. They had mugs of hot chocolate with his *mamm's* homemade marshmallows. It'd been a full day of laughter, food, and warm kisses when they were in his buggy.

After a quick knock on the shanty door, her younger sister Abigail peered inside at her. "I looked for you in the house, barn, and outhouse. I was worried when I couldn't find you." Abigail's blue eyes widened. "You've been crying."

"I came out here to be alone. I didn't want the family to hear me crying." She pulled Abigail inside the small shanty.

"I miss Justin so much. We would've been married now and living with his parents and family. I'd looked forward to being Justin's *fraa*."

Abigail hugged her. "I can't imagine what you're going through. I wish none of it had ever happened."

Before her brother had moved out to get married, she'd shared a room with Abigail and another sister, Molly. Her sisters got their brother's vacant room. Isabella thought Abigail was the sweetest sister and pretty with her honey-blonde hair. If she left home to have the baby, she'd miss Abigail the most in her family. Although she was only two years younger than her age, she couldn't burden her sister about having a baby.

"I keep hearing it was God's will, but I don't see how that could be. Why would He want to take a young man like Justin who was on the verge of getting married?"

"I don't know but I'm thankful that you survived the accident." Abigail said in a gentle voice, "Bad things happen to good people all the time. If you ever need to talk, I'm available to listen."

"*Danki.* That means a lot. I'll miss you if I leave home."

Abigail frowned. "Why would you leave?"

"I feel lost living here. Nothing feels right any longer. I had looked forward to starting a new life." Isabella shrugged. "Don't pay any attention to me. I'll eventually work things out."

"What do you have to work out? Is there something you aren't telling me?"

Should she tell her sister about the baby? Would it help to get her feedback about what to do? Maybe later, she might share with her, but the problem was Abigail's opinion of her would change. *Abigail looks up to me and whenever she needs advice, she always asks me.*

She took Abigail's hand in hers. "We better head to the house to help with supper." She wasn't hungry but should eat for the baby's sake.

Once inside the kitchen, Isabella mashed potatoes while Molly set the table. Abigail sliced the meatloaf into pieces.

"Tom King is going to join us for Thanksgiving dinner," her mother said.

Did she hear her correctly? They hardly knew Tom. "*Mamm*, we barely have enough room for our family," Isabella said, glancing at their table. Tom was a big man with broad shoulders, and he had to be several inches over six feet. Their kitchen looked dingy, and the walls needed fresh coats of paint. "Why would you invite him?"

"I asked him when I learned he doesn't have plans for the holiday. His family is going away and he's staying home to take care of the livestock. He accepted right away." Her *mamm* gave a small smile. "I know it's too soon to think of courting, but he's *gut* husband material. You're young and will want to get married."

"Justin died last month. I'm not interested in Tom or anyone else. And he's older than I am." She shook her head. "First, Rebecca mentioned me marrying Tom, now you." To say she was annoyed with both women was putting it mildly. She understood that the Amish way was to have a widow or widower hurry remarry when they had young *kinner*, but she was not desperate to get married because of having a family. When her mother learned about the baby, she would try hard to get her married to Tom.

Was that the best for the baby even though she could never love Tom? And it was doubtful he would want to marry her. Even if he'd agree to marry her and raise her baby together, she never could become his *fraa*. How could she betray Justin by becoming another man's wife?

After supper was finished, Isabella felt ill. Fortunately, Molly and Abigail said they'd do the dishes. Sympathy filled Abigail's blue eyes. "You don't look well. I hope you aren't coming down with something. Go to bed and I'll bring you a cup of tea."

Isabella nodded at Abigail before she left the kitchen. She figured the stress of Tom coming to Thanksgiving had made her ill. Her stomach hurt a lot with her food feeling like it might come up. If she had to throw up, maybe she should go to the outhouse instead of going to her bedroom. She decided to go upstairs because in the closet there was a sick bowl.

Isabella slipped her prayer covering and apron off before she got under the bed covers. A few minutes later, Abigail set a steaming cup of tea on a saucer on her nightstand.

"*Daed* told *Mamm* that she shouldn't have invited Tom King. He said you need more time to grieve for Justin."

"That's something."

"There's more," Abigail said, sitting on the edge of the bed. "He misses Justin coming here to see you. *Daed* enjoyed talking with Justin and said he had a good head on his shoulders."

With a hand resting on her stomach, Isabell raised her eyebrows at that. "Justin had a way with people. He could find something to talk about with each person and brighten their day. Everyone liked him but it never occurred to me that *Daed* would miss him too."

"I'll let you rest." Abigail stood.

She sat up in bed and picked up the cup. "*Danki* for the tea."

After Abigail closed the door, Isabella glanced down at her chest, thinking how her breasts were fuller and felt tender. As she sipped her tea, she worried that feeling sick might occur daily after this episode. She knew some women didn't have morning sickness but felt queasy at other times during the first trimester.

She needed more time to figure out her plan of action. Telling her parents caused her a great deal of stress, but did she have the courage to leave her home to keep her secret?

If only I had someone to help me to decide what to do, but there is no one in my situation to offer advice. Lindsay was like me with no support and was young and pregnant. Her advantage was getting a college education and improving her life. I don't see myself doing that and trying to take care of a baby. Lindsay finally had her happy ending with the father of her babies. My story won't have a happy ending. Justin is dead.

Her chest tightened, thinking how the baby had changed everything. She regretted what she and Justin had done but it was too late now to change anything. It seemed many things were against her.

I will have money soon from the baby quilt. What a blessing that Lindsay asked me to make it. She wanted to pay me ahead for it, but I told her to wait until she saw the quilt. Tomorrow I'll call Hannah to get the message to Jenna about the quilt. When I receive the money, I can see how much a bus ticket will cost and pick a random place to go. I won't have to face my family with the truth. They know I am heartbroken at losing Justin.

There was a problem with her plan. Abigail would go to the bus station to learn where she'd gone. If she wasn't dressed as an Amish girl, the ticket employee might not be of any help to answer questions about her. She could experience *rumspringa* and dress as an Englisher. Of course, she wouldn't really be in *rumspringa* because she had joined the church. To get married they had to be church members, so she and Justin had joined a year ago. She talked about doing the running around time with Justin, but he wasn't interested in leaving Millersburg. The Swartzentruber Amish were not allowed to leave the community during *rumspringa*, so it was nice the Holmes County Fair was held each year in Millersburg. At least, she'd gone to the fair with Justin this past August and their friends, Luke and Hannah.

She could buy clothes at a Goodwill or a thrift store and conceal her identity. Her accent might give her away, but she would talk as little as possible when she purchased her ticket. It was a bit scary because she had never taken a long trip by bus or car. Her church district was restrictive in many ways, but she would live by her own rules when she left home.

Touching her stomach, Isabella realized the pain was less.

After Jenna took her to the obstetrician, she would catch the bus to somewhere where she couldn't be found and live a different life until the baby was born. She would pray for the perfect couple to adopt her baby. Lindsay found Katie and Roman Yoder on her road trip to adopt Jenna and Amy. It could all work out for her baby.

Even though she had a tentative plan, tears welled in her eyes and her heart ached. The ending she wished for could never happen. Sadness enveloped her soul thinking how she wouldn't have Justin and their baby in her life.

Chapter Ten

"I'm glad this is a short week of school. It's nice there aren't any classes on Wednesday."

Harris looked up from his skillet of eggs and watched her sip the one cup of coffee she allowed herself. She couldn't give up her coffee totally, so only drank it in the morning. "You sure you want to cook everything yourself." He put a plate of scrambled eggs and bacon in front of her. "We can order a family dinner. They even include the pies."

"Maybe some other time we can do that, but I want to cook this year. We'll have all three daughters here plus Eli, Seth, and your parents. I don't see this happening each year. And Phoebe is taking Wednesday off from work to help me clean and get ready for Thanksgiving."

Harris nodded, sitting next to her at the white granite countertop. He liked the kitchen remodeling job Lindsay had done. She had chosen white cabinets and a gray back-splash. Phoebe had picked the stools with the red seats. It was funny how similar her kitchen was to his former house in Cincinnati. When he reconnected with Lindsay, he'd been impressed by how well she'd remodeled her house on a teacher's salary. He was blessed to be married to the love of his life and to be a father to their adult triplets. So, it happened a little late in his life. Another blessing was Lindsay being able to get pregnant after having cancer. Glancing at her rounded belly covered with a coral top, he said, "You look beautiful."

"Thank you." She laughed. "I'm enjoying wearing bright colors to show off my new body shape."

"I guess we better not book the Hawaiian trip yet. Phoebe said Seth wants to plan their honeymoon." Although he understood Seth wanted to take care of the honeymoon, Harris thought the Hawaiian trip would be an awesome wedding present for the couple.

"I hadn't heard that but that's sweet of Seth."

"I talked to Phoebe this morning when you were in the shower."

She frowned. "I'm worried about Seth giving up so much to marry Phoebe. I never thought he'd want to leave his Amish faith. He's quitting a job he loves too. I don't want Phoebe to move to Millersburg but maybe she should look for a physician assistant job there. It seems like Seth is making all the sacrifices."

"I don't want her to move away. I like having one daughter close by." He stood and walked around the island. "I better hustle and get to work. By the way, I left my practice in Cincinnati for you and I have no regrets. I know it isn't the same with Seth making such a major change in leaving his Amish roots, but he seems to be happy."

She shrugged. "When Seth moved to a studio apartment in Millersburg, I was surprised. He didn't have much longer to be home."

He rinsed his plate and put it in the dishwasher. "Personally, I think it'll be good for him to live alone for a few months. He'll have to fix his own food and won't be under Katie's thumb."

She carried her plate to the sink. "You're right. It could be for the best. When Katie tried again to fix him up with Veronica, that was the last straw for Seth."

He grinned. "I have to reward you for saying I'm right." When he pressed her lips to his, she wrapped her arms around him, clutching him tightly. A surge of warmth went straight to his heart at her closeness. He loved breathing in the raspberry body spray she used. It was so Lindsay...sweet and refreshing.

After their passionate kiss, her beautiful smile was wide. "I like being rewarded by your kisses."

"Now I don't feel like going to work. I'm tempted for us to both play hooky and stay home."

She gave him a quick kiss on his cheek. "Hey, you better go to work. We have a baby on the way."

"I love hearing about our baby." He secretly hoped for a boy but having a girl would be special too, especially if she looked like Lindsay. "Take it easy at work today. I'm glad you'll be off for Christmas vacation."

"Me too because we'll be busy getting a room ready for our baby. I want the cradle in our bedroom for the first couple of months before moving him to his room. We have to move furniture around to make room for the cradle. Seth should get it done in January or before." She frowned. "We have a lot to do to get ready for Baby Manning."

～

As Harris drove to his practice, he thought how much better his life was since he learned Lindsay had given birth to triplets. At the beginning of learning the truth, he blamed himself a lot that he hadn't known she was pregnant. It wasn't all his fault. His fiancée Callie had intercepted and deleted the phone messages from Lindsay. He should've had backbone when his parents insisted Lindsay was a summer fling. Cutting off his money for medical school if he continued to see Lindsay was harsh, but he went along with what they wanted.

Before marrying Callie, he'd gone to Lindsay's hometown since he didn't have her phone number. When he saw Lindsay with Paul Prescott in the diner, why hadn't he gone over to talk to her? He was hurt when the waitress told him that Lindsay was married. But still, he should've gone to their booth and told them congratulations. Maybe she would've told him she was pregnant with his baby. That was all in the past. No point dwelling on the missed years of raising his triplets with Lindsay.

At least, she dared to contact him about the two daughters she'd given away and how she'd kept Phoebe when she was diagnosed with lymphoma. *I can't believe how Lindsay had to make a hard decision when she was a kid herself.*

Even though he liked Roman Yoder, it still bothered him that Lindsay had given Amy and Jenna to an Amish couple to adopt. He respected their simple life and their strong beliefs in staying separate from the world but thank goodness Phoebe wasn't going to become Amish. He knew Katie wasn't happy about Seth leaving their way of life to marry Phoebe. *Would Katie and Roman attend their wedding,* he wondered?

After he pulled into his parking spot, he prayed silently, *Thank you, Father, for all the blessings you have given me. Be with all my loved ones today and keep them safe. Help me as I meet with my patients and thank you for guiding me to join this practice.*

At a knocking sound on his window, he looked up and saw one of his younger partners, Sam. "I got you coffee and your favorite muffins."

"Thanks, buddy," Harris said, as he opened his door. "Are you buttering me up for some reason?"

"You're so suspicious when I do nice things for you." Sam shrugged. "Okay, I do want your opinion on one of my patients."

"I'll be happy to help." He liked Sam and appreciated his work ethic. Phoebe went out with him twice during a time when she wasn't seeing Seth. Sam had been disappointed when Phoebe decided she couldn't live without Seth in her life.

As they walked together to the building, Harris thought about how he was fortunate to find a practice to join after leaving his Cincinnati one. Hopefully, Seth would find a construction job in Columbus before he married Phoebe.

Late morning, Harris saw his last patient before lunch. He closed the folder after jotting a few more notes in the patient's file. When he heard his ringtone from his smartphone, he picked it up from his desk and answered it immediately when he saw it was Roman. He never called his cell phone. "Hello, Roman. Is everything okay?"

"Hi, Harris. It depends on how you look at it. Katie and I are disappointed that Seth plans on being baptized in Phoebe's Protestant church. It surprised us that he would do this. What do you and Lindsay think of Seth and Phoebe getting married? We want them to be happy, but we worry that Seth will regret his decision later."

Anger started to seep into his mind. *How could he think Seth would regret marrying Phoebe? So, it wasn't going to be an Amish wedding. Why couldn't they be more open-minded?* "We think a lot of Seth. He's an impressive young man. The important thing is he makes Phoebe happy. He's not going to regret becoming Protestant."

"When Seth is at your house for Thanksgiving, do me a favor and talk to him about how hard it will be in your world. Maybe he'll listen to you. I know Phoebe hates that she can't become Amish for Seth."

Had Katie told Roman to call him? This didn't seem like Roman, but his son leaving their faith might bother him enough to get help on their side. And Seth left home to live on his own. That must've been a shock to Katie and Roman, Harris thought. "They are both adults and haven't rushed into their decision to get married. I can speak to Seth, but I don't think it will make a difference."

"I appreciate you agreeing to talk with him. His grandparents are also disappointed and are hoping to change his mind when we see them on Christmas."

He cleared his throat. "I'm sure you remember my parents interfered in my life when I wanted to marry Lindsay. I missed out on knowing about our daughters. I regret that I wasn't able to raise them."

"They were wrong but us interfering is the right thing. We don't want Seth to ruin his life and Phoebe's. If she'd join our church, she'd have that in common with her sisters. Our family would be blessed with us sharing the same faith."

Harris tapped his finger on the desk. *I can't believe Roman feels so strongly about their upcoming marriage. Poor Phoebe and Seth. They should be able to do what they want.* "We share the same faith. We're all Christians and believe in Jesus Christ. That's the most important fact. Your family will be blessed with this marriage. Seth has accepted that Phoebe will never want to be Amish. He's gone ahead and received his GED and plans to get his driver's license soon."

"*Ya*, but many of our young people do this before they take their baptism instructions. They drive cars or trucks and might study and get their high school diplomas. They test the waters to see if they can commit to an Amish life. Seth never did any of this until now. I think he could decide to back out of becoming English."

Harris didn't see that happening but decided to keep quiet.

Roman continued, "Before I get off here, I want to ask about Lindsay. Is she feeling okay?"

"She's doing great and is happy to be in her second trimester."

"I'm glad to hear that." After a pause, Roman continued, "I better get back to work. Thanks for taking my call."

"Call me anytime."

Harris sighed, shaking his head. *Maybe it'd be better if Katie and Roman didn't attend the wedding. When the minister asks if anyone objects to the wedding, would Katie voice her opinion? Should he mention this conversation with Lindsay?*

He needed to eat lunch before his next appointment. Sam walked in as he moved away from his desk. "What to grab lunch?" Sam grinned.

"It'll have to be quick." He narrowed his eyes at Sam. "Why are you grinning at me?"

"No special reason. I figured it was a stupid question because you're always ready to get lunch."

They decided to walk where they could get subs close by and save time. Harris couldn't stop thinking about Roman's call. When Seth said he wouldn't join the Amish church, it had been a surprise. Seth was as Amish as they came with driving his buggy. He'd loved that form of transportation and many other things that were Plain. Although Harris knew Seth would never regret marrying Phoebe, he might in time resent giving up his faith for her.

"You seem deep in thought," Sam said after he gave his order.

"Phoebe's future father-in-law, Roman, called me. I wish he hadn't. He wants me to talk to Seth when he comes for Thanksgiving. He doesn't want Seth to become Protestant."

"That's understandable. Amish parents have strong beliefs when it comes to staying separate from our secular world. My grandmother was Amish before she married my grandpa. Her parents basically disowned her and said she wouldn't go to heaven."

"I didn't know that about your grandmother." Sam never had mentioned to him that he knew anything about the Amish. He'd known that two of his daughters were raised by an Amish couple when dating Phoebe.

"Yep, you learn something every day." Sam frowned. "Talking about them reminds me of Thanksgiving. I'll be glad when it's over. I guess I'll go to a restaurant to eat on turkey day."

"Why aren't you going home?"

"I would fly to Wisconsin if my parents were still hosting it but now my aunt is having it. I don't feel like making the trip to my Aunt Lucy's house. She talks constantly and she takes offense at anything said. That is when we get a chance to speak." Sam groaned. "And Aunt Lucy can't cook."

"I'll check with Lindsay but I'm sure you can join us."

"If it is okay, let me know if I can bring anything."

Chapter Eleven

After they prayed together, Lindsay glanced at the long table with enough room for all their Thanksgiving guests. She was disappointed that Helen and John were not celebrating with them. They were ill with coughs and colds, so they'd decided to stay home. They didn't want to expose the family to what they had. She was pleased with the great decorating job Phoebe did. There were small vases of orange and yellow flowers in the middle of the table. She added candles and seeing them burning brightly was nice with the cloudy day.

"Mom, everything is delicious," Amy said.

"It is," Sam said. "Mrs. Manning, thank you for including me for dinner."

Harris grinned. "Hey, I helped but Lindsay did a great job."

"Sam, please call me Lindsay," she said, smiling. "I'm glad you were able to come today." *As long as he doesn't flirt with Phoebe.* It was obvious Sam had a thing for her. She wouldn't be surprised if that was one reason he'd been eager to come to their house. "Phoebe and Amy helped, and Jenna brought the pies, so I can't take credit for preparing the whole dinner."

Harris asked, "Seth, how do you like having your new place?"

He wiped his mouth with a napkin. "I like it except I miss the workshop in my *daed's* barn."

"After you're married, you're welcome to use our garage or basement," Lindsay said. "That is if you live here in Columbus." She didn't want to act like she assumed that Columbus would become their home.

Amy frowned. "I don't blame you for moving to your place, but it's different with you and Jenna both out of the house."

Seth grinned at Phoebe. "What a fella does for love."

Sam stared at Seth for a moment. "You're making a lot of changes in your life. I hope it works out for you. My grandmother left her Amish family and said it was difficult."

"Thanks, Sam." Phoebe rolled her eyes at him. "I already feel guilty that Seth is the one making sacrifices." She sighed. "I wish I could've joined the Amish church, but I couldn't."

Jenna buttered her roll. "It's been a surprise that my sister is marrying my *bruder*, but I know their love is strong enough to face all the challenges."

Lindsay wondered how it would go when Harris talked to Seth about being baptized in the Protestant church. She wished it didn't have to be this complicated for Seth. Was it too much to hope Roman and Katie could accept their son's decision? She'd be glad when Phoebe and Seth were married and became settled in their lives.

"Amy, I heard you wanted to be a nurse," Sam said.

She shrugged her shoulders. "I did have that dream, but I'm not going to now. I'd have to go too long to become a registered nurse. It's okay because I love being an EMT. Also, I want to take my kneeling vows after the wedding."

"I thought I told you that, Sam." Harris looked around the table. "I'm proud of our daughters. They are doing awesome in their jobs."

Eli grinned. "I'm glad Jenna became an EMT. It's nice sharing the same career with my beautiful *fraa*."

"It does help us to understand what we each experience daily," Jenna said.

"Do you work together?" Sam asked.

Eli shook his head. "Not usually. At least, we work the same shifts sometimes so we can go to work together."

Lindsay heard Sam speaking to Phoebe about visiting their practice. He said that she might someday reconsider and decide to become a doctor. Why would he invite Phoebe? *It has to be to spend time with her.*

Phoebe put her fork down and looked at Sam. "I love what I do. Sure, I'd thought of becoming a doctor at one time, but I love being a physician assistant. I enjoy working for a general family doctor."

The conversation turned to what board game they should play. Seth suggested Sequence, and said, "Phoebe and I will be on a team."

Sam frowned. "I never played sequence."

"I know how to play. We can be on a team," Amy said.

"Let's first get the dishes out of the way." Jenna stood, carrying her plate and Eli's to the kitchen.

"Should we eat dessert now or wait?" Lindsay asked, noticing everyone was finished eating.

Harris grinned. "I can eat pie now and eat another piece later."

Lindsay said, laughing, "It's good we have plenty of pie then."

While Phoebe rinsed off the dirty dishes before placing them in the dishwasher, Lindsay said, "We'll use paper plates for the pie."

"I'm taking Isabella to the doctor tomorrow. I'll pick her up at Hannah's." Jenna slid a piece of pumpkin pie onto a plate.

"I'll pay for the visit and other expenses. I'll give you my credit card." While cutting the apple pie, Lindsay said, "I'm guessing she didn't tell her parents about the baby."

"I don't think she has. Otherwise, she'd see a midwife." Jenna paused, then continued, "Maybe not because if she did see a midwife, her condition would spread quickly through the Amish grapevine."

Amy said, "I'll make a fresh pot of coffee to go with the pie."

Phoebe put the detergent pod into the dispenser and started the dishwasher. "It's so sad Justin died. She's young to go through this pregnancy. I'm glad you both are helping Isabella."

"The baby quilt I had her make for me is beautiful. I'll show it after we eat our dessert." Lindsay felt sad, thinking about how she went through her first pregnancy without family support. She hoped Isabella would tell her parents. After their shock, she hoped they'd realize the baby was a miracle. Isabella didn't miscarry after the terrible buggy accident.

⁓

Harris hated asking Seth to join him in Lindsay's office, but he decided to be brief about changing religions. "I was asked to talk to you about committing to the Protestant faith. Are you sure you want to do this?"

Seth looked uncomfortable, sitting in a chair across from Harris. "Did my *mamm* ask you to talk to me? No, I imagine she had my *daed* ask you to do it."

Harris nodded. "Roman called me. They're concerned about you. I wonder if you waited to be baptized in our Protestant church if that would help ease their minds."

Raising his eyebrows, Seth asked, "You mean to have our wedding, then later I can join Phoebe's church? I don't think that will help any but it's a good suggestion."

"I don't like this tension for you and Phoebe, but I don't see it ending anytime soon. Maybe after you're married, Roman and Katie will be more accepting."

"I doubt it, but we can pray they will be." Concern filled Seth's green eyes. "I have to ask you about Sam. He seems too interested in my fiancée. He even asked Phoebe to show him around the neighborhood because he was thinking of buying a house. I suppose you'd rather have him for a son-in-law. He's educated and makes a good income as a doctor."

Harris shook his head. "I'm thrilled to have you in the family. You and Phoebe belong together. I'm not sure why Sam's thinking of buying a house. He loves his apartment."

"I trust Phoebe, but Sam is too clever. He's able to come up with ideas to try to get her interested enough to spend time with him."

Harris walked around the desk to Seth, placing his hand on his shoulder. "You're a smart guy. Phoebe chose to spend her life with you. I was put in a spot to talk to you, but I'm glad it's out of the way. Let's enjoy the rest of the day."

Chapter Twelve

"How was your Thanksgiving?" Jenna asked, turning her head to look at Isabella in the back seat. Last night, Phoebe drove them back to Millersburg. She stayed overnight at Jenna's since she'd had Friday off from work. Although it was great to have Phoebe drive them to Isabella's appointment, Jenna was relieved that Hannah's family wasn't home. It was hard to imagine that the Swartzentruber Amish wouldn't hire a car except in emergencies. She didn't want to cause trouble for Hannah by not driving her buggy to get Isabella.

"Not good since *Mamm* invited Tom King. She tried to keep us together all day. I thought Tom would never go home. I have no interest in marriage. I know it'd be good for the baby to have a father, but I can't see marrying Tom. He asked if he could take me for a buggy ride sometime. Of course, my mother immediately answered for me. She doesn't know about the baby, so I'm not sure why she's anxious to get me married."

Phoebe said, "I can see why you aren't thinking of getting married. But your mother must think she's doing the best for you by throwing you and Tom together."

"Parents can be interfering, but it sounds like your mother cares a lot. She wants you to be happy. It is too soon for her to do her matchmaking, though." Jenna continued, "We had an interesting Thanksgiving with Sam. He definitely wants to spend time with you, Phoebe."

Phoebe looked at Jenna while stopped at a red traffic light. "He got on my nerves. Sam's nice enough but he's so full of himself. I wish he'd accept the fact that I'm going to marry Seth."

Isabella noticed Phoebe's diamond ring sparkling from the sunlight hitting it. Her hand rested on the steering wheel. "Your ring's pretty."

"Thank you. I just got it yesterday. Seth surprised me with it because I didn't expect to get a ring. He even got the right size by taking my birthstone ring with him to the store."

Isabella suspected Phoebe thought that since the Amish didn't buy engagement rings, Seth wouldn't think to get her one. "When are you two getting married?" she asked.

"In March. I can't wait." Phoebe sighed. "I want to stay at my job in Columbus, but I'll look to see if there are any openings here in Millersburg. I feel guilty that Seth's making so many sacrifices."

"No one is forcing him to do it. He loves you," Jenna said.

Isabella cleared her throat. "Jenna, when you found out you were adopted, were you upset that Lindsay gave you away? If I put my baby up for adoption, I hope he won't feel unloved by me."

"We were shocked to learn about our adoption at age twenty-two." Jenna looked at Phoebe. "Another surprise but a good one was to learn we had a sister."

"I'm glad the truth finally came out, but I hate it was because Mom had cancer." Phoebe pulled into the hospital's parking lot. "She kept the adoption a secret because she'd promised Katie she would. She couldn't do it any longer because if she died, I would be alone. And Mom was anxious to find Amy and Jenna."

Jenna nodded. "*Daed* wanted to tell us the truth, but *Mamm* never wanted us to know."

"I didn't know Lindsay had cancer. It's nice she could get pregnant after going through that." Isabella unfastened her seatbelt. "Phoebe, you can go in with me to the appointment too."

"That's sweet of you. I'll stay in the waiting room." Phoebe smiled. "It's going to be fine. Jenna will take good care of you."

As the three got out of the car, Jenna said, grinning, "They will take a test and make sure you're pregnant. It's a routine thing even though we know you are."

"You'll hear the baby's heartbeat if you are at least six weeks pregnant." Phoebe continued, "That will be exciting. Mom was thrilled to hear her baby's heartbeat."

"I remember her telling us about her ultrasound when she was expecting us. When she learned that she could be pregnant with identical triplets, panic shot through her. She almost fell off the table from the shock. I'm glad she didn't." Jenna laughed.

⁓

Wearing a paper gown over her naked body was not enjoyable, Isabella thought. *An Amish midwife wouldn't have examined me like this during the first visit.* I wonder if the midwives at the hospital require you to wear a gown during the first exam. Jenna told her about midwifery at the local hospital, but she hadn't wanted to go back there for her check-ups where Justin had died. Jenna said the midwives were excellent and all had gone through training and examinations for certification.

She also thought it was safer to go to a private obstetrician to keep her pregnancy a secret. At least Dr. Sullivan was female, so that helped, and she smiled a lot. She was pretty with blonde hair and expressive, green eyes.

"Everything looks great. We should be able to hear your baby's heartbeat since you're seven weeks pregnant." Dr. Sullivan smiled as she moved her stethoscope around on her belly. "Here it is."

While listening to her baby's heartbeat, Isabella said, "I wish Justin could hear it too. It sounds pretty fast."

"That's normal for a baby's heartbeat," Dr. Sullivan said. "I'm glad you came today. You can get dressed and I'll see you in a month. If you have any questions before then, you can give me a call."

"Thank you." *I won't be seeing you in a month. I'll be living wherever my bus ticket takes me. I need to pay for this office visit. I hope it doesn't take too much of my money.* Isabella knew she had money saved from sewing for Lindsay. Her parents were unaware of her earning money. If they knew, she would be required to give them the money. It was doubtful they'd allow her to continue sewing for Lindsay. It was hard to keep it a secret, too, but it would be too difficult to explain how she even knew Lindsay. Her parents wouldn't be happy that Jenna was her friend and that she rode in Phoebe's car today.

After Jenna and Dr. Sullivan left the room, Isabella removed the gown. As she slid her black dress over her head, she thought how Phoebe looked lovely in what the Englishers called skinny jeans tucked into tall, flat-heeled black suede boots and a lavender jacket. It wasn't a heavy-looking jacket, but Phoebe said it was a thermal one and warm for the winter.

Swartzentruber Amish's rules were so different. Women could only wear dark-colored clothing, and she wore black because of grieving for Justin. It wasn't necessary to wear black when she wasn't a widow. But black suited her mood. Jenna's dress was blue. She wondered if Rebecca had stopped wearing the dark colors while living in Pennsylvania. She missed Justin's family and regretted not telling them about the baby. Would Justin have wanted his parents to know about the baby? Maybe after the baby was born, she could write to them. By then, it could be good news for them to have a grandchild.

At the sound of a knock on the door, she said, "Come in."

Jenna walked in and gave her a paper. "Here's a prescription for your prenatal vitamins. We can pick them up at the pharmacy before we take you back to Hannah's."

"I don't know. I need to have money to pay for this visit. I can get the vitamins later."

"My mom is paying for your visit. She insisted. You'll hurt her feelings if you don't accept her covering the cost. I'll pay for the vitamins. You're my friend and that's what friends do for each other."

"*Danki* for everything. I'll call Lindsay soon to thank her." She would have a lot of letters to write before she left home. First, of course to her parents so they wouldn't worry about where she was. She didn't want them to have the community look for her. She doubted they'd call the police because that wasn't their Amish way. She needed to write to Hannah, Jenna, and Lindsay. She would explain how she needed to get away because everything reminded her of Justin at home.

⁓

A few days later, Isabella's mother surprised her. She wanted her to go to Millersburg to get her several grocery items. Usually, her father went to the store the few times her mother needed anything. "Why aren't you sending *Daed* to go?"

"He left with Aaron to go to a horse auction."

"We don't need another horse." Her father couldn't even afford to paint the barn and house, but he had money to buy a horse.

Her *mamm* shrugged. "He might help Aaron to buy a horse. It's nice to have another man's opinion when looking to make a big purchase."

Isabella noticed her *mamm's* brown hair threaded with more gray hair. Was she the reason? It would hurt her *mamm* if she ran away from home, but knowing she was pregnant would upset her more. She could go to the Goodwill store and get the clothes for her disguise. When she left home dressed as an Englisher, her family wouldn't learn her destination. They would never guess she'd abandoned her Amish clothing. She could only go as far as her money would take her. She'd have to get a job and find a place to live. She hoped her school friend, Fern, could help her. She'd moved away after eighth-grade graduation to live in Cincinnati. Although she'd kept her address, she hadn't invited her to their wedding. She wasn't Swartzentruber Amish, so her parents discouraged her from inviting Fern. Now, it didn't matter. There hadn't been a wedding.

Her thoughts were interrupted by her sister, Abigail, entering the room. "Isabella, if you don't want to go to the store, I can."

"I want to go. It'll be *gut* to get out of the house and shop at the store for *Mamm*."

"I can go with you." Abigail grinned. "We can have sister time."

Her throat tightened. How could she go to Goodwill if Abigail went along? "I won't be *gut* company."

"It might be better for Abigail to go with you." Her *mamm* handed her the grocery list. "Leave now so you two get home before your *daed* does. He'll think I should've waited for him to go to the store."

As she glanced at the list, Isabella said, "*Ach*, he might not care. I see you have root beer extract listed. He loves his root beer." Her mother made tasty root beer a lot. "I remember you gave Tom the rest of the root beer. You were generous after he had just eaten here for dinner."

"He enjoyed it. He's single so doesn't have a *fraa* to make it for him." Her *mamm* went to the wood stove and poured a cup of *kaffi*.

Abigail grabbed her black winter coat off the hook. "I'll get the buggy ready for us."

"*Danki*." She was grateful not to have to hitch the horse to their buggy. She might not have morning sickness, but fatigue was an issue. "I'll go with you. I want to use the outhouse before we leave."

～

Once outside the grocery store, Isabella hitched her horse to a post, then she put a blanket over him for warmth against the chilly November air**.** "You can go ahead. I have an errand to run. I won't be long."

Abigail stared at her. "That's why you didn't want me to come to town. What errand is it you have to do?"

"I want to get some yarn to make something for Hannah. The craft store isn't far." Whew, she was relieved to think of an excuse but hated to lie to her sister.

Abigail rolled her blue eyes. "Okay, have fun picking out your yarn. If we get done fast, maybe we can get something to eat at a restaurant. This is the first time we have been in town by ourselves."

"That's true. How much money do you have? I guess we could share a dessert." Isabella wasn't about to spend any of her money on food.

"I have some money."

As soon as Abigail was in the store, Isabella found the Goodwill store down the street. It was close to the pharmacy where her prescription had been filled. It was a relief that she'd seen it the day of her appointment.

Before entering the Goodwill store, Isabella glanced around to make sure Abigail hadn't followed her. She rushed inside, feeling amazement looking at all the items. An older woman asked her, "Is there anything special you're looking for?"

"Clothes. Jeans and a top."

She smiled. "Oh, I bet you want to wear jeans in your *rumspringa*. I think it's nice you can experience something different before you join your church. We've had other Amish teenagers come here to buy clothing."

Isabella nodded, wondering if she knew any of them. "I'm not sure what size I need. I never wore pants before."

"I'll help you. You look about the size of my granddaughter and she wears a size 6."

She followed the woman to the middle of the store. "Here is a rack of jeans that should fit you. We have some cute tops too. If you need anything, let me know. I see someone standing at the cash register, so I better wait on them."

"*Danki* for your help." Isabella knew she needed to hurry and pick out her escape clothes. She wanted to hide her purchases in the buggy before Abigail saw anything.

Instead of getting the smaller size, she decided to go with one size larger in jeans. She picked up an orange blouse because she loved the bright color. Even though she was wearing black as a grieving fiancée, she felt it should be okay to buy the blouse.

～

"This is fun," Abigail said, looking around at the other customers in the restaurant. "I never got to do this in my whole life. *Danki*. We can't tell Molly. She'll be upset she wasn't at home and at Jacob's house. Their potato soup is *appeditlich*."

Molly had gone to help their brother's wife, Mary, to clean their house. Recently, she had a miscarriage, so Molly offered to go. She opened her mouth to tell Abigail there was another restaurant they should try. She'd enjoyed the cozy and cute restaurant she had gone to with Lindsay and Jenna. Thankfully, she remembered no one knew she went out that day when she was supposed to be at Hannah's house. "I doubt we'll get to do this again anytime soon, but I'm glad you suggested it."

"It's sad Mary lost the baby. She was excited about being in the family way." Abigail sipped her steamy cup of coffee. "I thought by now I'd be an *aenti*."

Isabella sucked in a breath. Could she share her pregnancy with Abigail? She'd be thrilled to be an *aenti*. *Nee*, it would be taking too big of a chance. It'd be a burden for her sister to keep the secret when she left home. Why did Justin have to die? Her eyes filled with tears.

Abigail put her cup down. "I'm sorry. I didn't mean to remind you of what you lost."

"It's okay. Justin and I were excited about getting married and having *kinner*, but God had other plans," Isabella said her voice breaking.

"Tom King is headed this way," Abigail whispered.

"Geez, you're right."

He towered over their table, removing his black hat. "Hello. This is a nice surprise."

Abigail smiled at Tom. "Isabella and I decided to get lunch before going home. The food is *appeditlich*."

"I went to the hardware store to get more nails. I'm repairing fences. *Danki* again for Thanksgiving dinner. I enjoyed spending time with your family."

Isabella nodded slightly, holding back from saying she hadn't wanted him at their holiday dinner.

"I eat here frequently. It's lonely eating by myself. I know you're in mourning for Justin, but maybe next year, you'll feel like coming here with me."

She didn't have the heart to tell Tom that would never happen. "*Ya, danki*."

"I better get my order in. I want to get back home to finish working. Enjoy your lunch."

Abigail said, "I'm glad you came to say hello."

After saying goodbye to Tom, Isabella took a bite of her sandwich. Her appetite had left her, but she didn't want to waste the food. She couldn't take it home and have her parents know they'd eaten at a restaurant when they had food at home. "That was awkward. He's a good-looking and nice man but I'm not interested in him."

"He is attracted to you. I wish he wasn't too old for me."

Isabella looked at Abigail. Her little sister would soon be old enough to attend singings. "He was only two years ahead of me in school, so when you're older, he won't be. Four years older might be attractive to you in time."

Chapter Thirteen

Two days later, Isabella slumped into a chair in her bedroom. With her head bowed and eyes closed, she prayed, "Dear Lord, what should I do now? I was stupid not knowing there isn't any bus station in Millersburg. I thought the hard part would be getting to the bus station in town. I want to go away and protect my family from knowing how Justin and I sinned. Forgive me for telling lies to Abigail about buying yarn when I wasn't. Please guide me in what I should do. I hate telling my parents about the baby. My *daed* will be angry. Thank you, Lord, that the baby has a strong heartbeat."

Although there was a bus station sixteen miles from Millersburg, she couldn't afford to pay a driver to take her there too.

Raising her head, she wondered, *How can I take care of a baby when I can't seem to do anything right? I'm glad I never wrote to Fern. She might have moved, and I don't know if that would've worked out in the first place. I don't know about going to Indiana, but I can't think of any place else. Eventually, they will realize I'm pregnant. I could stay there for a month, then find a place for unwed mothers. Jenna could help me. Or I can write to Rebecca and tell her I'm pregnant. She might invite me to live with them.*

She decided to talk to her mother and explain how she wanted to go away. She'd have to be convincing, so her mother wouldn't suspect it was something more than missing Justin.

Walking slowly down the stairs, she heard female voices from the kitchen. As she entered the room, the warmth poured through her. In the winter, it was nice to have a wood stove in the kitchen, but not so comfortable in the summer. Abigail stood by the stove while adding butter to the pan of potatoes.

"I've made your favorite supper. Meatloaf and Abigail's fixing the mashed potatoes." Her *mamm* finished putting plates on the table.

Abigail grinned. "I made a chocolate pie for you."

"Are you all right," her *mamm* asked, looking at her.

"It sounds *gut. Danki.* And I'm okay but I could be better." Fixing her favorite meal made her feel guilty to talk about leaving home but she had to do it now. It wouldn't hurt for Abigail to hear what she needed to say but hoped what she wanted to do wouldn't upset her mother. Feeling awkward, Isabella took a breath. "I'm having trouble moving on with my life because everything here in the community reminds me of Justin. Do you think I could go away for a few months to visit a relative?" She definitely couldn't say she needed several months.

Her *mamm* frowned. "I don't understand why you want to leave. You'll still miss Justin if you leave home. Here, you have family, Hannah, and others to support you."

Isabella shrugged. "I could go visit *Daed's* relatives. I didn't get to go when you all went to his cousin's funeral."

"I'll think about it but doesn't make sense to me that you'd want to go there." She put her hand on Isabella's arm. "I won't invite Tom again to our house. I realize that was a mistake having him here for Thanksgiving."

She hated her *mamm* thought it was because of Tom. It wasn't just about him but everything. "It's okay. I know you meant well. I'll get the glasses out for the root beer. I'm sure some will want your root beer, *Mamm*. When is Molly coming home?"

Abigail laughed. "I think she likes being with Mary and Jacob. She has her own bedroom."

As she poured the root beer into the glasses, Isabella thought, *I'll call Jenna soon. Maybe I can live with her. I doubt I can do anything else. She'll want me to tell my parents about the baby to see what they will do first. One thing for sure is they won't be pleased. I want to know if I can live with Jenna and Eli before I tell my parents.*

Dear Lord, give me the courage to do the right thing for my baby.

⁓

Jenna looked at Eli across the table but couldn't tell him that what she'd prayed for wasn't going to happen. She took a sip of her coffee, wondering why God hadn't blessed them with a baby. Being pregnant for Christmas would've been the best gift for her and Eli. Once again, she'd started her period. Moving to their own house and not living with her stressful mother-in-law hadn't made a difference in her fertility.

"You make the best pancakes."

"*Danki.*" She grinned. "Better than your *mamm's*?"

"*Ya*, definitely. Yours are light and sweet."

Earlier, she heard Isabella's message on the answering machine. She wanted to talk soon with her and said it was important. Had she told her parents about her pregnancy? If Isabella had, were they going to send her away? "I need to reach out to Isabella somehow. It's hard to contact her. She doesn't want me to call their neighbor's phone."

Eli frowned. "I thought she has you call her friend's phone."

"I called Hannah's phone, but I couldn't leave a message. It was full."

"When we get to work, you can try again."

She nodded. "I'll do that."

Shortly after, Eli and Jenna arrived at the hospital. While Eli took care of their horse, she climbed out of the buggy. Isabella rushed to her. "I'm glad you're here."

"Have you been standing out here waiting for me? It's cold outside." Jenna put her arm around Isabella's shoulders. "Let's get inside the hospital. I got your message and called but Hannah's machine was full. I couldn't leave a message."

"I hope you have a few minutes. Tom King brought me." Isabella blurted, "I know I shouldn't have used him for a ride, but I couldn't wait any longer to see you. I've been praying. And I have to ask you something."

Once the automatic doors opened, they entered the well-lit lobby. A couple of nurses paused by Jenna, smiling. "Good morning."

She smiled back and said, "Good morning." Jenna glanced around and saw an empty couch with no one nearby. There was a vase of flowers on the table in front of the couch. "Let's sit here. Eli and I came early, so take your time."

"I can't raise my baby. I went to Goodwill and bought jeans and a top. I planned on taking a bus and going away. I decided to tell everyone that I needed to get away because everything here reminds me of Justin. That part is true. Then I would return after I gave birth and give the baby up for adoption. I messed up. There isn't even a bus station in Millersburg. I can't do anything right."

"I'm sorry but I'm glad you aren't leaving." Jenna thought how scary to think of Isabella leaving home when she'd been protected from the outside world. She was too young to go off by herself with little money. She doubted her mother's money for sewing was enough to live on her own.

"After praying, I thought of a solution. I wonder if you and Eli would want to adopt my baby, and if I could live with you during my pregnancy." Isabella's urgent voice was filled with emotion. "I'll clean your house and cook. I won't be any trouble. I can sleep on the couch or anywhere you want me to."

Jenna's heart slammed into her chest, realizing she could be a mother to a precious baby. She hugged Isabella and said, "I'll have to talk to Eli, but I'd love to have you live with us and adopt your baby." She grinned. "You won't have to sleep on a couch. You can have your own bedroom."

"*Danki* so much. I'll tell my parents soon, but I don't see them wanting me to keep the baby." A wistful smile touched her lips. "Or wanting pregnant me around them. I'd be a bad influence on my younger sisters. And they'd be embarrassed to have the community know."

Jenna thought it was hard to know how they would react. It seemed unlikely they'd want her to stay at home to have the baby, but she wanted to be positive for Isabella. Her parents had been unfriendly when she'd met them in the hospital, especially Mr. Miller. She grasped Isabella's hand in hers. "They might surprise you. If you change your mind about the adoption, I'll understand. I have to tell you that this is an answer to my prayers. I have wanted to have a baby. I'm so *froh* that you thought of me to adopt your baby."

"My baby will be blessed to have you for a mother." Isabella bit her lower lip. "Do you think I can wait until after Christmas to tell my parents? I'd like to be home for it. I hope I won't show yet."

Jenna nodded. "That sounds like a *wunderbaar* plan for you to enjoy Christmas with your family."

"Do you think Eli will agree with you about adopting my baby?"

She saw the tension on Isabella's face and wanted to reassure her that adoption would be fine with him. "*Ya*, I'm sure he will. He'll love your baby too."

Isabella leaned forward. "I feel like a huge burden has been lifted from me. *Danki*, Jenna. I better go. Tom came over yesterday to see my *daed*. I asked him then if he could bring me here. I asked him not to share this with anyone. We're going out for breakfast. He's waiting in his buggy for me."

Although she was excited to share the adoption news with Eli, worries entered her mind. *Will Isabella change her mind about Tom? He obviously cares about her. Would they marry? I can see him accepting her baby and raising it with Isabella. I need to be prepared to accept whatever happens.*

～

"Did you get accomplished what you wanted to do?" Tom asked, holding his coffee cup.

Uneasiness floated through her body at his question. Isabella wanted to be any place else. After talking with Jenna, she'd considered canceling their breakfast plans but knew that would be rude. She shouldn't have involved Tom and waited to talk to Jenna. Her *daed* would be angry at her leaving with a single man so early in the morning. She'd have a lot of explaining to do to her parents. "*Ya*, I did. Jenna was the EMT on the scene when...the accident happened."

"I saw she's Amish. It's interesting how her church district allows her to be an EMT. Well, our faith wouldn't allow it for the women."

"Our Swartzentruber faith is limiting, especially for women. It'd be nice to be free to do more than stay at home." *Saying this viewpoint of me wanting to do more outside the home might discourage Tom from pursuing me.*

He raised his eyebrows. "*Ach*, are you thinking of becoming an EMT?"

She shook her head, surprised that he even could think such a thing. Working in a bakery or a fabric store might be something she'd want to do. She would enjoy getting out of the house and making money. "*Nee*. If Justin hadn't died, I'd be *froh* to be at home with him. It's been hard to adjust to life without him."

Compassion filled his eyes. "I'm sorry. It shouldn't have happened."

"I never expected Justin's family to move. I was excited to become Justin's *fraa* and to live with his family."

"I was surprised they moved to Lancaster, but I hope it works out for them."

"They won't have as many restrictions. Abe's parents are Old Order Amish." She opened the strawberry jam packet and used a knife to spread it on the buttered toast. "*Danki* for driving me to the hospital and for breakfast. I appreciate your kindness. I hope I can get in the house without any words from my father. I'm sure he'll say I could've eaten at home instead of you taking me out to eat breakfast." She glanced around the large restaurant. "Well, I see a few other Amish individuals eating here."

"Your father didn't return my wave when I picked you up." He grinned. "You rushed out so fast to the buggy that I didn't have a chance to talk to him."

"I'm sorry but I needed to talk with Jenna. I didn't want him to stop me from leaving." *I'm sure Tom's wondering why I had to see Jenna in private.* Guilt flooded her that she couldn't tell him the real reason for making him drive her on a cold winter morning to the hospital. "I'm afraid I can't tell you why I had to see Jenna. My parents don't know I'm friends with her. They wouldn't approve."

He winked at her. "Maybe someday, you'll trust me enough to tell me your secrets."

Chapter Fourteen

Jenna hadn't had a chance to talk to Eli because an emergency call was received from Toni Robertson. She hadn't called immediately because she assumed the chest pain was from heartburn. When they arrived at her house, her face was gray. Joe listened to her heart and took her blood pressure. He said, "We're going to get you on a stretcher and take you to the hospital."

"I'm giving you an aspirin to chew," Jenna said to Toni before they carried her out of the house.

"Okay," Toni murmured.

Once inside the ambulance, Jenna did tests, and five minutes out from the ER, she called ahead a brief report. She told them about Toni's EKG results, what treatment had been done, and her vitals. Precious time would be saved while the emergency room doctor reviewed and assessed the tests. Seeing Toni experiencing difficulty breathing, Jenna inserted a nasal cannula to provide her with oxygen.

Jenna said a silent prayer for Toni as the sirens blared. Heart disease was the number one killer among women, so Toni did the right thing to call 911. Hopefully, there wasn't a lot of damage to her heart.

Upon arrival, Joe called dispatch that they were there at the ER. Their driver, Chad, got out and opened the rear doors while Jenna and Joe removed the stretcher from the ambulance. After entering the entrance, Joe and the ER staff helped to slide Toni off the stretcher onto the hospital bed. Jenna gave a detailed patient report to the nurse admitting Toni. The ER doctor immediately came to take care of the patient.

Before leaving to return to the ambulance, Jenna smiled at Toni. "You're in great hands."

"Do you think Chad started cleaning out the medic truck?" Joe asked Jenna, as they left the ER. Grinning, he said, "Or is he saving that job totally for us?"

"I'm sure he's busy cleaning. Chad likes to get it done, so we'll be ready to go for the next call." Jenna knew they'd still have to roll up wires, restock medications used, and replace batteries.

As the automatic hospital doors opened for them, Joe said, "Hey, tell Amy hello for me. I might not see her. She's working a later shift today."

Poor Joe didn't have a chance with Amy now that she'd decided to join their church. It was too bad that he wasn't Amish because her sister had a sparkle in her brown eyes when he was around her. "Okay, I'll tell her." She turned to him with an amused expression. "Is there anything else you want me to tell Amy?"

Joe ran his fingers through his dark brown hair and was quiet for a moment. "I'd like to take her out on a date, but don't mention that."

While working in the ambulance, Jenna thought back to the time they lived in Shipshewana. Amy had strong feelings for David, but her best friend, Rose, married him. Amy hadn't been interested in any man since him except now Joe had attracted her attention. Unfortunately, he was off-limits with being an Englisher. If things were different, Joe and

Amy could marry and have beautiful babies together. *Oh my gosh, I sure have babies on my brain.*

—

Eli and Jenna sat at a table in the hospital cafeteria eating their lunches. Usually, Jenna packed their lunches, but they agreed to buy them today. After she swallowed a bite of her chicken salad sandwich, Jenna leaned forward in her chair. "What do you think about us adopting Isabella's baby?" After they had found their seats and prayed, Jenna told Eli about Isabella's visit to see her and how she asked her to adopt her baby.

"I can see why she wants you to be the mother. You're the perfect woman to adopt her baby, but I think Isabella seems very immature." Eli shook his head. "Why in the world would she have someone drive her to the hospital early in the morning to ask you to adopt her baby? She easily could've waited until you took her to the next doctor's appointment. Or she should have talked to you on the phone. She still has months left before she has the baby. What was her rush?"

Jenna realized what Eli said was true, but Isabella seemed anxious to have a plan in place for her baby and she was a teenager. "It's not easy to connect by phone with her, but you're right about her not being able to wait to talk to me." She lifted a spoonful of soup to her lips. "It was especially a surprise to see she asked Tom King to drive her here. Her mother tried to fix her up with him. Even Justin's mother said he'd make a good husband for her. Isabella has insisted she isn't interested in marrying Tom."

Eli fingered his sandwich. "That's what she says now. I hate to see you get your hopes up, then Isabella decides to marry Tom, so she can keep the baby."

"This tomato basil soup is good." She sighed. "I thought of that possibility too. I'd love for us to adopt her baby. But

I'm not sure her parents will want us to adopt their grand-child."

He wrinkled his face. "Because we are EMTs?"

She shook her head. "That probably is one reason, but it's also because Swartzentruber Amish don't think much of Old Order Amish. They feel we aren't really Amish because of the way we live."

"I knew they will only marry other Swartzentruber Amish." He sipped his coffee. "She needs to tell Justin's parents too."

Jenna exhaled a breath. "There's more why she felt a need to talk to me. She planned to take a bus and not wear her Amish clothing. If anyone asked if they'd seen an Amish woman, she would be dressed in English clothing. She went to Goodwill and bought jeans to wear for whenever she left Millersburg. She planned to write to her parents about how she missed Justin too much. That was her excuse for running away. After her baby was adopted, she'd come back here. That way no one would know she had been pregnant."

"That was a stupid idea," Eli said, looking annoyed. "How could she have enough money to support herself? I know Lindsay has been paying Isabella for sewing things, but that wouldn't last long."

She pushed her *kapp* strings off her shoulders. "Isabella didn't think it through and that is why she became upset. When she found out there isn't a bus line here in town, it was overwhelming to her. Isabella realized she definitely couldn't raise a baby when she messed up on her escape plan. Asking me to adopt her baby gave her a way to cope with her solution and to relieve some of her stress."

"It's good she didn't leave."

"I feel adopting her baby might be in God's plan for us. Maybe that's the reason we haven't been blessed with our own baby."

"We might still have a child of our own. I was sad you had two miscarriages. I know it broke your heart too. I still have hope you'll get pregnant again and there won't be a miscarriage."

"But what if I don't get pregnant again? Adopting Isabella's baby might be for the best. We'll finally have a baby."

"We haven't been married long enough to think it can't happen for us." Eli smiled at Jenna. "I guess I'm not enough for you. I want to have *kinner*, but it's nice to spend time with just you. I'm glad we could move out of my parents' house. I love my *mamm*, but she can be a bit much. It's great having privacy."

I better not mention Isabella wants to live with us. That will hamper our privacy, but having a baby would be wonderful. I don't need to tell Eli until Isabella is sure that is what she wishes to do. Jenna nodded. "I'm thankful all the time that we could buy our house." She reached across the table to squeeze his hand. "You're definitely all I need. I love being your *fraa*."

"Hi, you two," Amy said, taking a seat across from them at their table. "Did you have a busy morning?"

"Joe and I had a couple of calls." Jenna grinned. "He wanted me to tell you he said hello."

Amy gave a slight laugh. "That isn't necessary now. I came in early because he wanted to eat lunch with me. I'm waiting to meet him."

"I see now why Joe offered to take a later lunch." Jenna glanced at Eli. "Also, he knew I wanted to eat with my handsome husband."

Eli smiled his boyish smile at her compliment.

"You look pretty. I see you got your sewing done on your new dress." Amy wore a cranberry dress, and her lips were pink and shiny. *She must have put on lip gloss.*

Amy raised her eyebrows. "Don't read too much into me wearing my new dress. My other dresses were dirty. It's just lunch. It isn't a real date."

Standing, Eli said, "I'll leave so you two can chat. I have paperwork to get done anyhow."

Jenna nodded. She hoped to have a chance to tell Amy about Isabella before Joe came. "Isabella came this morning to see me."

"Is she okay?"

"She couldn't wait because she wanted to ask me to adopt her baby." Jenna told her about the conversation and how Isabella felt adoption was the best idea.

"What did you tell her?"

"I told her I wanted to adopt the baby." She sighed. "Eli doesn't want me to get my hopes up in case she changes her mind. She might decide to keep the baby."

"And she might not. She's young without a husband, so I think you could have a baby in your arms next year," Amy said, offering encouragement. "And I'll be an *aenti*."

"I like how you think." A warm glow of satisfaction settled in the middle of her chest. Her life was *gut* but adding a baby to their family would enrich their lives. She just needed to convince Eli.

Chapter Fifteen

Seth stood back, looking at the decorated tree. The Amish never had Christmas trees in their houses because it was considered too fancy and vain. He liked this English tradition but if his parents came to visit them in Columbus during the season, they would be dismayed to see a tree. "This is the first Christmas tree for me. I like the miniature lights and the pine smell."

Phoebe said, smiling at him, "I never had my own tree, so it was fun decorating it together." She laughed. "I'm glad I only had enough room for a small tree. It took longer than I thought it would."

He put his arm around her and kissed the top of her head. "Your apartment's nice and definitely bigger than my studio apartment." Phoebe's two-bedroom apartment consisted of a nice-sized kitchen that was open to the living room.

"You won't be there very long. Would you like to eat the Christmas cookies I made?"

He grinned. "*Ya*, I thought about sneaking a couple earlier."

"I'll get the cookies and make decaf coffee. It's too late for caffeine."

"I'll make the coffee." He went to her Keurig on the kitchen counter and turned it on. While it heated the water, Seth looked at Phoebe. Her shiny, black hair touched her shoulders. She looked beautiful in her jeans and pink sweater.

"Let's curl up on the couch. It'll be comfy." She carried the cookies to the coffee table in front of her dark blue couch with several red throw pillows. When her cell phone chirped, she went back to get it from the kitchen table. "It's a text from Sam."

He clenched his jaw when he heard Sam's name. What was with this guy? Why didn't he realize that Phoebe was not available? "It seems a little late for him to text you."

Frustration filled her brown eyes. "It is. I don't know whether to text him back or ignore him. I'm not sure why he's obsessed with me. I don't give him any encouragement that I'll ever be interested in him. I've told him that I love you."

Seth said, "You're beautiful and smart, but he has no business texting you. It's not like he has to stay in touch about work. I can text him and tell him it's me and I'm here with you."

"I don't know what we should do. I didn't want to involve Dad, but I'll have him talk to Sam to leave me alone."

"If you're thinking of going to Harris, Sam's been bothering you a lot, hasn't he?" He delayed making the coffee, wishing Sam would grasp the fact that he wasn't going to break them apart.

She nodded. "I'll ignore his text. Of course, I've done that before, and he still persists to text or call me. It's crazy how you had to deal with Veronica, and I have Sam not getting my message."

"I wouldn't say anything to your dad. He might want you to be with Sam. Is it okay if I text him?"

She drew in a deep breath. "It could be better if you text him. Dad thinks a lot of you, so you're wrong about him thinking I should be with Sam instead."

"Well, he did invite Sam to Thanksgiving."

"Just because Dad invited Sam to Thanksgiving dinner doesn't mean anything. Sam hinted around that he didn't have any place to go for the holiday." She widened her eyes at him. "Was that why you gave me my ring on Thanksgiving because of Sam?"

"I thought about waiting until Christmas, but I already had the engagement ring. I was anxious to give it to you. You do like it, right? The jewelry woman said we could exchange it if you wanted something else."

Phoebe held up her hand to look at her ring. "Are you kidding? It's stunningly perfect. I absolutely love it. I love you."

When he went to buy her ring, he wished that there was a woman to go with him. He couldn't ask his sisters. They wouldn't be any help because Plain women never wore jewelry. Amish never bought engagement and wedding rings for their brides. When an Amish man married, he was required to grow a beard. No rings for Amish men either. "I love you. I need to get the message across to Sam to leave you alone. I'll text him now, so we can enjoy the rest of our evening."

After he got Sam's number from her, Seth typed, *I'm here with Phoebe. Please stop texting my fiancée. She doesn't want you to continue to text her or call her.*

No texts came from the phones while Seth made the coffee. He put the mugs on the table and said, "If we hadn't met, would you have considered dating Sam?"

Phoebe looked startled. "Never. He's controlling and full of himself. I learned that when I went out with him a couple of times when you and I broke up for a few months. I'm glad Mom kept me. If we had been raised as siblings, I'm afraid you wouldn't have fallen in love with the Amish Phoebe."

He took a frosted sugar cookie and thought for a moment. "That's tough because I can't imagine you being Amish."

Phoebe sipped her coffee. "Obviously, I can't either."

"Maybe you fell for me because I was this incredible Amish man." Grinning, he continued, "Do you still love me as much now that I'm an Englisher?" He ran his fingers through his hair.

She nudged him and said, "I love you even more. You're still the same great guy I fell in love with while you were living an Amish life. I can't wait until our wedding."

"We could move up the wedding date to February. You have your bridal gown. We have chosen our attendants." He was happy that a friend, Corey, from Millersburg, would be his best man. Haley's husband, Scott, would be the other groomsman. "We met with the minister once already, so hopefully we can get the other two required meetings in before a February wedding."

"We'll need to check to make sure there aren't any weddings booked in February. Haley's and Scott's anniversary is in February. They're going to a resort in Cancun to celebrate. I'll check and see when they are going. We should order our wedding invitations soon."

"I've been thinking that we should go to Hawaii for our honeymoon. And we can celebrate your birthday in Hawaii. That is if your parents still want to give that for a wedding present." He hadn't realized how expensive engagement rings could be, but he wanted to get Phoebe a nice one. They had their wedding bands, but Phoebe had paid for his. Then he bought a used car after he got his driver's license. He would have to rent a tux for the wedding too. All these expenses were making a dent in his savings.

At least, Amy had bought his buggy and horse from him, so that gave him extra money. He was grateful that she did because Amy would take good care of Ace. It'd been hard giving up his buggy and Ace. Living in the apartment was okay, but he eventually wanted them to buy a house in the country with a few acres.

She gave him a puzzled look. "I thought you wanted to be in charge of the honeymoon."

He chuckled. "Scott told me that I shouldn't turn down a trip to Hawaii."

"I can help pay for our honeymoon, but you can still plan it."

"No, you shouldn't pay for any of it." He'd feel like a loser if she paid some of the honeymoon expenses.

"We can go to Hawaii. It'll make my parents happy to do it for us. I'll tell them to book it as soon as we know our wedding date."

"I might have a construction job here to start in the spring, so you won't have to support me."

She gasped, grabbing his hand. "That's exciting. When did you find out about the job?"

"I received a call while we were shopping for gifts. It's not definite. I have to go for a second interview."

"You'll get the job," Phoebe said with confidence. "I'm sorry I couldn't find a position for a physician assistant in Millersburg. Then you wouldn't have to start a new job. I know you like the guys you work with and have been there for years."

"It's okay. I know you want to be here when Lindsay has her baby."

"Are you sure you'll like living here in Columbus?"

"I can live anywhere as long as I'm with you." Smiling, he said, "Well, maybe not in Alaska."

"You're so precious to me." There was a gentle softness in her voice.

Her sweet voice did him in and he had to kiss her thoroughly. Taking her in his arms, he first kissed the tip of her nose, then her eyes, and finally, he kissed her soft mouth. Her lips were warm and moist with the taste of coffee. His breath hung in his throat at her nearness, and his heartbeat accelerated. Mixed feelings surged through Seth when she drew his face to hers in a renewed embrace. He wanted to make love to Phoebe but knew it should be saved for their wedding night. They'd made it this far without giving in to temptation, but it wasn't getting any easier to remain chaste.

When they stopped kissing, Seth said in a defeated voice, "I better go get a motel room."

Confusion crossed Phoebe's lovely face. "I thought you were going to stay here. I have two bedrooms. We have such little time together."

"It'll be too tempting for me to stay overnight."

"We can behave. I'll be in my bedroom, and you can sleep in the guest room. In the morning, I'll make breakfast for you."

"I don't know. I guess but I don't want your parents to find out I spent the night."

"I definitely don't want your parents to know either. I can't wait until we're married, and I wake up to you every morning." She gave him an impish grin. "You're right. We should move the wedding to February. I'll talk to Haley, Amy, and Mom tomorrow."

"I'll talk to Corey about it too."

"What about your parents?"

"Amy can tell them we might change the date." He decided not to tell Phoebe that it was doubtful any of his family would attend an English wedding. Well, Jenna and Eli would and of course, Amy since she was a bridesmaid. He couldn't see his grandparents making the trip for their wedding.

"You don't think they'll attend, do you?" Raising her chin, she looked him straight in the eye. "I wish we could have your bishop and my minister do the ceremony together. Then they would come."

After a quick kiss to her lips, he said, "That's a nice thought, but I'm afraid the bishop wouldn't agree to participate in a Protestant ceremony. We can send invitations to my family. My *Aenti* Lizzie might come." She'd told him recently that God was everywhere and not just in their Amish faith. But living a simple life and putting God first was essential.

"I don't understand why they can't attend when you haven't been baptized in the Amish faith. They are practicing shunning if they don't attend. It's like they are disrespecting our church wedding. If I had become Amish, I'm sure my family would've attended our wedding. They attended Jenna's and Eli's."

~

Seth rearranged the pillow behind his head. He couldn't get comfortable in the guest room. Too many thoughts were running through his head because Phoebe was so close. He hated seeing her upset but he definitely couldn't go to comfort her. It was hard to restrain himself around her. *I hope we can change our wedding date to February. I can't wait to make love to my beautiful Phoebe.*

Miriam would be a person to ask for help. She'd gone to her adopted son's English wedding. Could she convince his parents to go to their wedding? It'd be awkward to ask for her help since she was Veronica's mother. Knowing Veronica, she might have told Miriam about how he led her to believe he was interested in her. That was so far from the truth, but he couldn't share how Veronica was delusional and they never had a relationship. No one else came to his mind to ask for advice. *I don't even know if Eli and Jenna will be at our wedding, but I'd think they would attend. They are EMTs so they're exposed to a lot of situations.*

Seth knew what he needed to do. He should pray to God and give Him the worry about his relatives breaking Phoebe's heart and his by not attending their wedding. He thought about the Bible verse in Peter and how he should cast all his worries upon the Lord. He folded his hands in prayer.

"Dear Lord, please soften my parents' hearts and other family members, so they will come to our wedding. Give me the right words to explain to them how much we want them to be part of our celebration. I know they're disappointed in me, but I hope they can forgive me for my decision to marry Phoebe and to leave the faith they raised me in. Thank you for bringing Phoebe into my life and for all the blessings you have given me. In Jesus' name, I pray."

Chapter Sixteen

Isabella touched her baby bump, knowing today she'd tell her parents the truth. Christmas was over. It couldn't be put off any longer. She was three months pregnant, and it'd be better for her to tell them now. Maybe she should've told them earlier, but she wanted to be home for Christmas. After they learned about her baby, she couldn't imagine they would allow her to remain living at home.

I won't mention that Jenna said I could live with her and Eli. Maybe they'll help me to think of a solution. Hopefully, it won't be to marry Tom. It could be someone else because, after breakfast with Tom, Daed had slapped her face hard for going out early with him. Justin would have been a wunderbaar-gut father. She couldn't imagine him hitting their child in the face. His discipline would've been done in love and not in anger.

She would never marry someone just to give her baby a father. It seemed impossible to her to love again after losing Justin. It would break her heart to give their baby away, but adoption should be the best thing to do.

Fortunately, Abigail and Molly were at a friend's house, but they would be home later in the day. Isabella heard her parents talking in the kitchen, so she left her bedroom to face them. As she slowly took each step on the stairs, her heart raced. Will my father slap my face? Or will he tell me to leave home immediately?

"I need to tell you both something." She drew in a deep breath, standing at the end of the table where her parents were drinking kaffi. "I'm in the family way."

Her mamm's mouth dropped open. "Ach, I can't believe it. That's why you've been so tired."

"Is Tom King the father? I'll get him now and you two need to see the bishop and make plans to get married."

Isabella grabbed the top of a chair to brace herself. "How could you think that Tom would be the father? I'm three months pregnant. Justin is the father."

Her mother clenched her jaw, then stared at her husband in a fiercely manner. "What are you thinking? Even I know that Tom wouldn't be the father."

"We only slipped up once and when I realized I was pregnant, it was a relief that we'd be getting married soon. Justin talked about confessing to the bishop but then the buggy accident happened." She wouldn't mention that she'd disagreed with Justin about confessing to the bishop.

Her daed shook his head, looking stunned. "I can't believe Justin and you did this. You both knew better. Didn't you ever listen to the sermons about not giving in to your desires before marriage?"

"Ya, but it happened anyhow. We regretted it but if Justin hadn't died, we wouldn't be having this conversation."

She hoped her mother would get off her chair and hug her. That won't happen, she thought. Daed seems too shocked to hit me.

Her mother frowned. "You should've told us before now. I'm guessing the hospital people knew you were pregnant after the accident."

Isabella nodded. "Ya. I might as well tell you that Tom took me to the hospital the morning I left early. We did have breakfast. I told the truth about that, but the main reason to go was I wanted to talk to Jenna. She was one of the EMTs at the accident. Tom doesn't know I'm pregnant."

"Please sit down, Isabella." Her mother pointed to the chair by her. "I understand now why you asked to go to Indiana. You said it was because being here, you missed Justin so much, but it was to hide your pregnancy from us, wasn't it?"

"I told the truth about it being hard to live here. I miss Justin all the time, but I planned on running away and never telling you that I was pregnant. I was planting the idea in your head so when I left, you'd think it was only because I missed him so much. Then I'd give the baby to a nice couple to adopt and return home. No one would know that I was pregnant with Justin's baby."

She jumped when her father hit the table with his hand. "I can't believe you've been sneaky about everything. What were you thinking? Go to your room so we can figure out what to do. I hope you didn't tell your sisters."

"Nee, I didn't." She stood and said, "Jenna said I could live with them. That's why I went to the hospital. I wanted to ask her if she would adopt my baby. She and her husband haven't been able to have a baby." She decided to get it all out in the open. She wasn't going to wait and see where they sent her.

"That is never going to happen." Her daed glared at her. "They aren't like us. I can't believe they claim to be Amish. You've already shamed us enough. I don't want them to adopt your baby."

"Did you tell Rebecca and Abe? Maybe you can visit them. It shouldn't be just on us to figure this out." Her mamm rubbed her chin. "Our first grandchild and we have to deal with you not being married. Babies are blessings, but not like this. I never thought you and Justin couldn't wait until your wedding night."

"I went to tell Rebecca but too many people were there to help them move." She sighed and continued in a sad voice, "I knew it would be hard for her to hear what Justin and I did. He was like the perfect son to her."

"No one is perfect except Jesus, but I know what you mean. We all loved Justin." Her mamm touched her arm. "You're too young to reject getting married."

Tears filled her eyes at her mother's words. Justin was perfect to her. He could never be replaced in her heart by another man.

~

Two days later, Isabella left a message for Jenna to cancel her doctor's appointment. Her parents wouldn't allow her to go to Hannah's, so she didn't see how she could see the obstetrician. She decided not to tell them Hannah knew about her pregnancy. It was unlikely Jenna could pick her up at home for her appointment because her father would chase her away. She wished it would be possible to tell her mamm how Jenna and Lindsay had been sweet and support- ive to her. It'd hurt her feelings that she'd shared with strangers about her pregnancy first instead of telling her own mother.

I'd love to tell how Lindsay coped with having triplets and gave two of her daughters to an Amish couple to raise. It was nice hearing how Lindsay had her happy ending fi- nally with Harris. All those years she'd never married but still supported herself and Phoebe. I don't know what kind of a job I could ever get, so I could raise my son or daughter. I only have an eighth-grade education. As precious as it'd be to keep my baby, I don't see how it could happen.

After the supper dishes were finished, Abigail and Molly worked on a puzzle in their small living room. They'd asked her to help them with it, but Isabella saw her parents motion to the stairs. "I'm tired but danki for asking me." While climbing the stairs, she knew her parents had decided what to do about her shameful condition. It had to be that she'd be sent away, but where to?

Within a few minutes, her mamm knocked lightly on her door and Isabella said, "Come in."

Her mamm sat on the edge of her bed and patted a spot next to her. After Isabella sat beside her, she said, "I remembered a dear friend of my mother's. We visited her before my mother died. Martha's a widow and has agreed to have you live with her. Your daed will hire a driver to take you to the bus station. He'll go with you and see you off."

Isabella couldn't speak for a few moments. She hadn't been asked if she wanted to go to this woman's house. "Where does she live?"

"Martha lives in Michigan. You can help her with household chores. She uses a cane to get around. We'll say how it'll be nice for Martha to have you visit. She doesn't have any kinner so I hope it will work out for both of you."

"Will I see a midwife there?" If she had to leave, it'd be nice to see a midwife instead of a doctor, even though Dr. Sullivan had been kind to her.

"Ya, she knows a gut one for you to see."

"What if I refuse to go?"

Her eyebrows rose. "Isabella, you have no choice. You need to have a positive attitude about going."

That was another reason I wanted to leave this house and live with Justin and his family. I'd have felt like a complete person married to Justin. My feelings would've mattered.

Her mamm continued, "We aren't sure what to do about contacting Rebecca and Abe. They have a right to know about their grandchild, but Abe's health isn't gut. Also, we're afraid they might tell someone in our community. Rebecca has close friends here. Just hold off on writing to them."

"I doubt Rebecca would blab to anyone. It'd reflect poorly on Justin in her eyes." She knew it wouldn't help but decided to express her opinion. "I'd rather live with Jenna and her husband."

Her mother's expression softened. "I know you would, but you'll like Martha. She knows of a couple who might want to adopt your baby. They've been disappointed that they don't have any kinner. Ach, they are Swartzentruber Amish so that's a relief."

"I'll go but it feels weird to stay with someone I've never heard of before. It'll be uncomfortable to live with Martha."

"It's the best situation we could think of for you." She briefly touched Isabella's arm. "We aren't sure which day you will leave. Your daed has to get a driver to go to the bus station. He needs to check the times for trips to Kalamazoo, Michigan."

"Could the driver take me there instead? You could go and visit with Martha."

"I hadn't thought of that. I'll see what your daed thinks. I doubt he'll want to drag this out because he wants to get it settled as quickly as possible. It might be too hard to get a driver to take us to Michigan. And he isn't froh about getting a driver. He'd rather drive the buggy but it's too far to go for our horse and to come back immediately." Her expression sharpened. "You should've told us earlier instead of waiting. We might have been able to come up with another plan."

Sure, get the pregnant daughter out of the house as soon as possible, she thought. But it was why I waited to tell them. I understand it'd be too embarrassing to have me stay in my condition.

"I want to say goodbye to Hannah before I leave."

"Don't tell her that you're in the family way."

She wondered if her brother, Jacob, would learn about her pregnancy. He and Mary were anxious to start their family. It'd be hard to hear about her expecting a boppli when they were married and no kinner yet.

After her mother left the bedroom, Hannah came to her mind. She'd miss her a lot. She'd asked her to be a wedding attendant. Hannah's boyfriend, Luke, was to be one of Justin's attendants. They'd been an awesome foursome at the singings and laughter had erupted from them at the youth gatherings. Playing volleyball on these evenings had been a lot of fun too. Those times with Hannah and Luke were over now. Tears rolled down her cheeks. How could she have ever survived this ordeal without her friend? Hannah never hesitated to help her and tried to comfort her after Justin's death.

I'll slip outside to the shanty soon to call Hannah and see if I can visit her tomorrow. I can't wait because I won't be here much longer. While at her friend's house, she'd contact Jenna to ask her if she would still want to adopt her baby. If she did, maybe she could live with Jenna during the last couple of months of her pregnancy. Her eighteenth birthday was in March. She'd make her own decisions then. She'd stay with Martha during her second trimester but would move back to Millersburg before she had the baby. She liked the idea of Jenna and Eli being Old Order Amish. Her baby would grow up with fewer restrictions but still be in an Amish family. She didn't agree with the belief that they were not Amish enough.

Chapter Seventeen

Jenna hated to hear Isabella's sad voice. Although she was glad Isabella's parents knew about her pregnancy, she hated they planned to have her go out of state to have the baby. "Would it make any difference if I talked to your parents? If you stay with us, they could visit you."

"I wish that would be possible. They would prefer I'd stay with Englishers rather than Old Order Amish which is weird. I know they don't want me close to home either. Someone from our community might see me if I lived with you."

Jenna knew how the Swartzentruber Amish felt about their Old Order church, so she wasn't surprised. There must be someone whom Isabella could stay with, so she could continue her pregnancy visits. "Maybe they would allow you to stay with Phoebe then. She's definitely English. It would only be until she gets married in February so that probably wouldn't be that helpful."

"I thought Phoebe and Seth were getting married in March. Not that it matters because I doubt they would allow me to stay with Phoebe."

"They moved it up a month. Instead of March, it's the first Saturday in February. They put a rush on their wedding invitations, so they can get them sent out soon."

"That's nice. I hope the weather will cooperate for them, and there won't be any snow."

Jenna knew Isabella had done great during her first trimester but decided to ask about her health now. "Are you still feeling fine?"

As the silence grew, she became worried. "Isabella, what is it?"

"I hate to mention that I've been pretty sick. I started throwing up on Second Christmas and it has continued. I still can't tolerate any food. I think knowing I had to tell my parents the truth caused it to start."

"*Ach*, that's terrible. You did so well before. You and your baby need nourishment. I should take you to see Dr. Sullivan."

"My parents haven't noticed that I'm sick. We don't have a bathroom in the house, so I've been lucky I can get outside in time."

"It sounds like it's stress related, but we won't know until you see the obstetrician." Jenna hoped that there wasn't anything seriously wrong with Isabella and the baby.

"I've never been away from home except for going to Indiana to see relatives, and going to Michigan terrifies me. I won't know anyone, and Kalamazoo is a big city." Isabella gave a little laugh. "I haven't taken a bus anywhere. If I had done my original plan and escaped on a bus, I never would've gone to a big city. Justin and I talked about going to Sarasota, Florida, sometime. We thought it'd be fun to take the bus and enjoy the beach. It'd have been an adventure we hadn't experienced."

"That would've been a nice trip. I'm sorry you didn't have more time with Justin." Jenna thought for a moment. "I could go with you on the bus if that helps any." What was she getting herself into? Eli might not want her to travel to Michigan.

"To tell the truth, I'm surprised my *daed's* getting a driver to take me to the bus station. We never ride in cars unless it's a big emergency. I guess he's rattled by me being pregnant. They would be upset if they knew I'd ridden in a car with Lindsay and Phoebe."

"When are you leaving?"

"They haven't said but I'm guessing early next week after New Year's Day. I doubt *Daed* knows off the top of his head whom to call to drive us to the station."

"If you're too sick to travel, you should tell your parents."

"I'll try to, but they might not believe me and could think I'm using it for an excuse to get out of going to Michigan."

"If you still go, will you have access to medical care? Does Martha know a midwife for you to see?" The only reason Isabella hadn't wanted to see a midwife before was to keep her pregnancy a secret. She only went to an obstetrician in Millersburg because it was a private practice.

"*Ya, Mamm* said Martha knows a midwife for me to see."

"I can have your medical records sent to the midwife."

In a breathless voice, Isabella said, "I better get off here soon. I hear Hannah's *mamm's* voice. Maybe she needs to use the phone before they visit her sister. The only reason I got to come here is because I wanted to tell Hannah goodbye before I leave for Michigan. Abigail drove the buggy because my *daed* said he was busy. Thanks for listening."

"I'm going to get you a cell phone, so you can call me whenever you need to. I've thought about getting one before with you having to go to Hannah's place at times to call." Also, Jenna realized Michigan winters might be colder than Ohio's. "And you won't have to walk in the winter weather to a shanty."

"You don't have to do that. The fresh air is *gut* for me, but I appreciate you wanting to buy a phone for me. I hope Martha has a phone for me to use." Isabella moaned. "I wish

I didn't have to go there. I don't even know her. My mother hasn't seen her for years."

"I'll keep praying for you. I wish your parents would allow you to live with us, but if you continue to be ill that might help them to see you really can't leave your home."

"I turn eighteen in March, so I plan on leaving Michigan then. If you'll still have me, I want to live with you during the last trimester. I hope you'll still want to adopt my baby."

"We do want to adopt your baby." She wasn't positive about Eli being completely on board yet but knew he would be once he met Isabella. He'd see what a sweet girl she was.

"I better go."

"I'll keep praying for you."

After Jenna ended the call, she wished with her whole heart that Isabella's parents would change their minds about Michigan. *I'll call Mom to see what she thinks I should do. I feel like going to Isabella's house to check on her in another day or so.*

The cold wind ripped through her as she walked back to the house. Maybe Ohio was just as cold as a Michigan winter. A slight pain went through her left wrist which had been broken from a buggy accident. When it rained, she felt pain there too.

It'd happened soon after Amy and I learned we were adopted. Poor Seth blamed himself for having us go with him to make home deliveries. The accident wasn't even my brother's fault. Amy broke her ribs but because of our injuries, we spent two awesome weeks with Lindsay and Phoebe in Columbus to recover. It was a time for me and Amy to bond with our biological mother, father, and Phoebe. I can't imagine not having them in our lives.

Eli met her at their back door. "I was getting ready to check on you. How's Isabella?"

She ruffled his dark blond hair, thinking how Isabella's baby might be blond like Eli and have blue eyes. "I'll make coffee. I'm cold."

"We can drink coffee, but I know another way to warm you up." Grinning, he pulled her into his arms. "I haven't kissed you thoroughly this morning."

Her heart gave a little thud. "I like how you think."

He lowered his head and kissed her. She closed her eyes, savoring his kiss. Being cold was not on her mind with her warm husband hugging and kissing her.

"I love you," Jenna said, as she eased her mouth away from Eli's lips. She wondered if she would ever get used to the emotions swirling inside her whenever Eli kissed her.

"I love you more," he replied quickly.

She said, grinning, "You're so predictable but I love how you always respond with loving me more."

"*Ach*, really. I'm predictable now. For that, you're going to be sorry." Eli tickled her side with gusto.

She laughed so hard that finally, she yelled, "Stop it."

His blue eyes flashed at her with amusement. "I haven't tickled you for ages. That was fun."

"When we do have *kinner,* hopefully, they will be ticklish.*"*

Eli cupped her face and ran his thumb over her cheek. "Why would you want that for them?"

"So, you can have fun tickling them." She winked at Eli. "You did warm me up but I'll make coffee for us."

"I'll get the cookies you made." Eli went to her cookie jar that was a wedding gift from her *Mammi* and *Daadi.* "I have something to tell you."

She turned the gas burner on under the teapot to heat the water. Then she put heaping tablespoons of medium-ground coffee into the French press pot. Opening the cabinet door, she pulled two mugs off the shelf.

Eli munched on an oatmeal raisin cookie. "Your cookies are *appeditlich.*"

She sat at the table by him. "Coffee will be ready soon. What do you want to tell me?"

"If Isabella wants us to adopt her baby, I think we should. I've been praying about it and feel you're right about adoption."

Incredulous, she stared at him. *Now that things didn't look hopeful, he's interested in adoption. Not just adoption, but Isabella's baby.*

He gave her a concerned look. "What's wrong? Did she decide to keep her baby?"

"*Nee*, but her parents want her to take a bus to Michigan and there is a possible Swartzentruber Amish couple there interested in adopting her baby. Isabella has been throwing up for days. I'm worried about her. I don't see how she'll be able to travel. I think the stress of leaving is making her ill."

"What can we do for her? Should we go visit her? Or would that make the situation worse for Isabella?"

She shrugged and walked to the stove. Lifting the teapot, she poured the hot water into the coffee pot and stirred with a wooden spoon. She put the plunger in and said, "I don't know what to do. She still wants us to raise her baby, but her parents don't agree. They consider us too liberal."

After a few minutes, Jenna poured the coffee into their mugs. As they sipped their hot drinks, Eli said, "This coffee's *gut* and flavorful."

She nodded and took another sip. Deep in thought about what they could do, she absentmindedly picked up a cookie. "We could take cookies to the family and fruit for Isabella to try to eat. I don't think they would object to that. If we hurry, she might still be at Hannah's, and we can avoid her parents."

"I'm glad we both have today off from work."

⌒

As they pulled into the driveway, a younger version of Isabella rushed out of the house to their buggy. "I was going to the shanty to call you. Isabella fainted and she hasn't gained consciousness. I'm Abigail."

Fortunately, Jenna had thrown a medical bag in the buggy. She grabbed it, following Abigail into the house while Eli stayed behind to quickly tie their horse to a post.

"I moved Isabella to her back. What do you think caused her to pass out?" Abigail asked. A flicker of worry appeared in her blue eyes as she looked downward at her sister.

She squatted on the floor next to Isabella. After she saw that her friend was breathing, and didn't see any injuries, Jenna answered Abigail, "I'm guessing she's dehydrated so that caused her to faint." She couldn't mention Isabella's pregnancy also had something to do with her fainting. Abigail might not realize her sister was expecting a baby.

"I'll get a glass of water for her, but should I call 911 first?"

Jenna glanced at the young woman with vivid green eyes, looking around the same age as Isabella. "You must be Hannah. How long was she unconscious?"

"Maybe a couple of minutes."

"If she doesn't regain consciousness soon, 911 needs to be called. A glass of water would be helpful."

Eli entered the room and asked, "Is there anything I can do?"

"I wish she'd regain consciousness." Jenna lifted her legs above her heart level to aid the blood flow to the brain.

Eli removed the blood pressure cuff from the bag. After he took Isabella's blood pressure, he said, "It's low."

After a moment, Isabella's eyes opened, looking dazed. "What happened?"

When she attempted to sit up, Jenna said, "Don't sit up yet. Take it easy. You fainted. I don't want you to faint again."

"You scared us." Hannah gave a glass of water to Jenna. "We were talking and suddenly you passed out."

"We need to get liquids in you." Jenna smiled at Isabella. "You didn't need to faint to get Eli and me here to see you. We were on our way to visit you."

Jenna put her arm around Isabella's shoulders as she slowly sat up enough to drink water.

Isabella said, weakly, "I feel so dizzy."

"I think it's necessary for you to go to the hospital. There you can get an IV in you for fluids. You were unconscious for longer than I like. You haven't been able to eat so that's another reason you need to go."

Eli nodded, removing his cell phone from his pocket. "I'll call."

Chapter Eighteen

Jenna couldn't believe Isabella was on her way to the hospital but knew it was for the best. Things had rapidly gone downhill for the young mother. She'd forgotten Amy was on the schedule, so it was *gut* for her to be in the ambulance with Isabella. She could take care of admitting her. Jenna needed to talk to Abigail and Hannah while Isabella was transported to the hospital.

"I'll call both of you with updates about Isabella." She looked at Abigail. "And you can tell your parents. I suppose it's better if it comes from you about Isabella's fainting and being unconscious."

Abigail said, "I'll tell them. Even though they will be upset she's in the hospital, I'll make them understand the seriousness of her condition. I'm glad you and your husband came. It was scary for us to see her faint." She bit her lower lip. "What made you come?"

"I talked to Isabella on the phone. She told me how she hasn't been able to tolerate food." Eli put his arm around her shoulders. She smiled at him, appreciating his support.

"My sweet *fraa* wanted to hurry come here to see Isabella. We hoped she'd still be here."

"But why did she call you?" Abigail raised her eyebrows, looking flustered. "I remember her mentioning your name when the buggy accident occurred. I feel like there is more that no one is telling me."

Hannah said, "Isabella has been keeping a secret, but it's time for you to know it. She's pregnant. She wasn't far along when Justin died."

Abigail sat on the nearby couch. She looked like she'd lost her best friend. "I can't believe she never told me. I thought we were close. Did Justin know before he died?"

Hannah nodded. "*Ya*, he knew. He felt guilty about it."

"Do our parents know? I'm guessing they do. *Mamm* and *Daed* have looked miserable."

Hannah nodded. "She told them recently, so that could be why she's been stressed. They want her to go to Michigan to keep her pregnancy a secret."

"Isabella and I became close. I took her to an obstetrician. I'm sure there were times Isabella wanted to tell you, but she wanted to be able to stay home as long as possible." Jenna realized there was a lot that Abigail hadn't known. It was better not to mention that she might adopt Isabella's baby.

"She told me because Jenna picked her up here and knew she couldn't go to your house. She also felt safer using our phone since we don't share it with neighbors." Hannah touched Abigail's shoulder. "I know Isabella wanted to tell you the truth, but she thought the fewer people knowing about her pregnancy would be better."

Jenna saw the hurt was still on Abigail's face that she'd been left out of Isabella's secret. In a low voice, Abigail said, "She could've trusted me to keep quiet."

Eli asked, "Hannah, how are your parents with this situation?"

Hannah frowned. "They don't know that Isabella's pregnant. I'm glad they are at my *aenti's*. Will she be at the hospital long? I wish I could visit her."

"She'll have to get liquids in her now because she's dehydrated. Once she tolerates food, she should be released." Jenna looked at Eli. "We better leave and get to the hospital."

Abigail stood and put her coat on. She covered her *kapp* with a larger black bonnet. "I need to leave too. I dread going home to face my parents."

As they all three went to the door, Hannah said, "I'll pray for Isabella and for you, too, Abigail."

"*Danki*, Hannah," Abigail said.

"Hannah, I appreciate all you've done for Isabella. You're a good friend." Jenna hoped she wouldn't get into any trouble for helping Isabella. When she'd picked up Isabella at Hannah's house, her parents thought she was visiting her friend, not going to the doctor about her pregnancy. The Millers might blame Hannah for the deception if they learned how involved she was in helping Isabella.

"I wish I could've done more. It's been difficult on her with losing Justin." Hannah gave a grateful smile. "You've been amazing and a real blessing to Isabella. God put you in the right place when she needed an understanding person in her life."

Jenna got a lump in her throat at hearing Hannah's kind words. "*Danki*. I'll be in touch."

Abigail walked with them to their buggy. "Is the pregnancy the main reason Isabella fainted?"

Jenna looked at Abigail. "Some women faint while pregnant with the changing hormones, but being dehydrated and weak from not eating were factors too. I'm glad you're aware now that Isabella's pregnant."

"I never thought this would happen to Isabella, but everything would've turned out so differently if Justin had lived." Abigail let out a long breath as she looked at Jenna and Eli. "I wish I could go to the hospital with you but I better go home."

Jenna hugged Abigail. "I'll tell her you want to visit. She might not be in the hospital too long."

Eli helped her in the buggy and within minutes, they were on the way to the hospital. Jenna was quiet as she tried to process all that had happened. Although she knew Isabella would get the medical care she needed, would her parents change their minds about having her go to Michigan? She wanted Isabella to move in with them, so she wouldn't be stressed. How could she convince Isabella's parents to allow her to live with them? It seemed impossible.

"Are you warm enough?" Eli turned his face away from the street to look at her. "You've been quiet."

She glanced down at the blanket on her lap. "I have been deep in thought apparently. I see my thoughtful *ehemann* put a blanket on my lap and turned the heater on. Despite the low temperatures, I'm nice and warm." She was thankful they had a battery-run heater for their buggy. "I'm worried about Isabella and her parents' reaction to her being in the hospital."

"Her trip should be delayed." He patted her arm. "It might even be canceled."

She shrugged. "But then what? They don't want her condition made known in their community."

"We can see if she can move in with us, but it's doubtful her parents will allow it."

"I guess we can try."

⁓

Jenna saw Dr. Sullivan outside Isabella's hospital room. "You got here quickly."

Dr. Sullivan ran her fingers through her curly, blonde hair. "I just delivered a baby girl." Grinning, she continued, "A great way to start the day. Isabella is hooked up to an IV. I'm glad you called 911. Amy gave her hard candy to suck on. Plenty of my patients claim that sour hard candy, especially the fruit-flavored kind, helps settle their stomachs. I'm hoping to get her to tolerate food by tomorrow. Although nausea can occur in the second trimester, it isn't common."

"I'm not sure what Isabella told you, but she's been under a lot of stress. Her parents want her to move to Michigan."

"I knew she'd told her parents. I'm glad you and Amy are here for her." When her pager beeped, she said, "I better go. Sounds like an emergency."

Jenna wasn't surprised to see Dr. Sullivan using a pager instead of a smartphone. Many doctors still relied on pagers because dropped calls occurred in the hospital hallways when using a cell phone. With more broadcast power, paging networks worked better with signals to penetrate buildings. Different doctors had told her that sending group messages were received nearly instantaneously. In an emergency, if a patient has no pulse, then a staffer would need to notify a full team of medical personnel quickly.

Jenna entered the room and saw Isabella was awake. "How are you?"

She turned her head to look at Jenna. "I feel weak. *Danki* for coming to Hannah's house. I'm worried about not being able to eat. I hope I can keep food down soon."

Jenna moved a chair next to Isabella's bed, glancing at the IV. "Abigail wanted to visit you, but she needed to go home to tell your parents where you are."

"I'm sure she had questions. Does she know I'm pregnant?"

"Hannah told her."

Isabella's blue eyes clouded with sadness. "I should've told her, but I knew I'd lose her respect. A little sister should have a big sister to look up to."

"She was hurt that you hadn't confided in her, but she loves you. She's a sweet girl. It's *gut* for you to have another person to support you, and Abigail will."

"It's hard being here because this is where Justin died." Isabella's voice came out hoarse.

"I'm sorry." Jenna couldn't believe she'd never thought that the hospital would be a source of pain for Isabella because of Justin's death. "I admire you. You've had a lot to deal with but you're strong. You'll get through all this."

"I should've called you earlier and told you I was getting sick. On Christmas Day, I couldn't stop thinking about Justin. I missed his family too. I wish they hadn't moved to Lancaster. I felt so lonely even though I was with my siblings and parents." She sighed. "How was your Christmas?"

"We went to Shipshewana for Christmas. We have a lot of relatives, including grandparents there and friends."

"That's right. I remember you, Amy, and Seth grew up there."

Jenna nodded. "We celebrated Christmas early with my biological parents and grandparents. Second Christmas was spent with Eli's family." She liked how their faith celebrated Second Christmas on December twenty-sixth. The Amish set aside this second day to continue the Christmas celebrations of exchanging gifts, enjoying delicious food, and visiting families.

"That's nice you were able to fit everyone in." Isabella cleared her throat. "I seem to create more expense. I hope I don't have to stay long. At least, the driver who hit Justin's buggy paid the hospital bill from the accident."

Jenna wondered if he paid the bill to help his case when it went to trial. "Don't worry about the cost. Just get better." Looking at Isabella's wan face, Jenna knew she shouldn't stay long.

"What do you think my parents will do now? I'm not happy I fainted but maybe something *gut* will come out of it. They could decide not to make me go to Michigan."

Jenna nodded. "I hope so. If it's okay with you, I'd like to say a prayer with you."

"I'd like that."

She gently grasped her hand. "Dear Lord, be with Isabella as she strives to get better. Help her to be able to eat food without getting ill. Guide Isabella's parents in making the best decision for her once she's well. We give you praise for everything and the blessing of Isabella's and Justin's baby. Fill us with the joy of the Holy Spirit. In the Name of Your Son, Amen."

Isabella's eyes misted over. "That was beautiful. I feel special in the Lord's eyes after your prayer."

"You and your baby are special. I want you to get some rest. Would you like to have a piece of candy now?"

At her nod, Jenna stood and opened the bag of candy. She handed a piece to Isabella. "I told Abigail and Hannah I'd call them. I'll be back tomorrow to see you."

"I am tired. Jenna, I love you."

"I love you too. Now close those beautiful eyes."

Jenna felt drained but in a nice way. She'd been touched by what Isabella had said. As she walked to find Eli, she wanted more than anything to help Isabella through her pregnancy. Even if Isabella decided to keep her baby, she wanted to be part of her journey.

"Are you looking for someone?" Eli asked.

"*Ya*, a good-looking EMT. Do you know of one?"

He chuckled. "I might."

"*Ach*, I feel like I let Isabella down, but Christmas was a busy time. I never thought how hard it would be for Isabella with missing Justin and knowing she had to face her parents with her pregnancy."

"You didn't let her down. You're the one suggesting we should go to her house today. It turned out to be a wise decision." Eli took her hand in his. "Let's get out of here and get something to eat. You always feel better after you eat."

She made a face at him. "*Nee*, you're the one who feels better after eating, but that sounds great."

Chapter Nineteen

Lindsay had a small, empty plate and a glass of lemonade by her. Everyone had brought appetizers to the New Year's Eve party at Eli's and Jenna's house. She'd eaten the vegetables and spinach dip and a few other snacks. Everyone was seated at the dining room table, playing Uno. There were red candles around the room, drifting a cinnamon spice scent to her nose.

Phoebe sat across the oak table from her, wearing a mid-length gray dress with a red jacket. Her black, shiny hair touched her shoulders in waves. Lindsay felt underdressed, wearing maternity jeans. However, she redeemed her outfit with her sparkly silver blouse. Jenna looked pretty, too, in her cranberry-colored dress and white *kapp*. It was sweet how the triplets had grown close despite their differences. She wished Amy had been able to make it to the party. At least, they'd see her tomorrow.

Harris nudged her arm. "Hey, sweetheart, I think you might want to say something."

Realizing she only had one card left, Lindsay yelled "Uno." The game quickly ended when she discarded her one remaining card in the next round. She had the required five hundred points, so the game was finished.

Phoebe walked around the table gathering the cards to put away. "Congratulations, Mom."

"I have a prize for the winner. I think you'll like it, Mom. Does anyone want dessert?" Jenna asked, rising.

"I'll take a piece of your *mamm's* coconut cream pie," Roman said. He patted his belly and chuckled. "I saved room for it."

Katie glanced at her husband. "After we eat dessert, we should head home."

"I thought the store is closed on New Year's Day," Seth said. "You can stay with us to see the New Year in."

"The store is closed but we never planned on staying until midnight." Katie grinned. "We aren't as young as all of you."

"You're not old," Phoebe disagreed.

"*Danki.* That's nice to hear."

"You don't look your age, *Mamm*, but now *Daed* is a different story," Seth said.

"*Ach*, you have aged me, Seth." Roman smiled at Katie. "You look like the beautiful woman I married."

Katie shook her head, smiling back at her husband. "Always the charmer. Phoebe, I'm glad you're spending the night, so we'll get to spend more time with you and Seth tomorrow." Sipping her coffee, "I don't usually like decaffeinated coffee, but it tastes great. Amy should be back tomorrow from Shipshewana. She wanted to visit with Rose and David."

"It's supposed to snow after midnight, so another reason for us to leave soon." Roman pushed his chair away from the table. "I'll get a refill of coffee. Harris, you want anything?"

"I think I'll take a little piece of cheesecake and Katie's pie. I need to stretch my legs, so I can get it." Harris smiled at Lindsay. "Do you want to share my dessert?"

Lindsay gave a slight laugh. "Stop it. I seldom take any of your food. I'd like a small piece of cheesecake."

Harris wore dark blue jeans and a Henley, long-sleeved shirt that she'd gotten him for Christmas. It was funny how Seth also wore jeans except his were faded, and he also wore a Henley shirt that Phoebe gave him for Christmas. Phoebe had gone shopping with her. She'd remarked that Seth would look good in the shirt.

Seth's transformation to the English world seems complete in many ways, Lindsay thought. *He isn't wearing Amish clothing any longer. He even bought a used car after he got his driver's license. He does have his high school diploma now and just needs a job in Columbus. What a relief that Phoebe and Seth haven't mentioned they moved their wedding date up to February. Avoiding talking about the Protestant wedding is for the best, so they can have a peaceful night with the family. I hope Roman doesn't corner Harris in the kitchen about the wedding.*

Jenna brought her a mug of coffee. "I thought you might like coffee with your dessert. It's decaf. Dad's got your cheesecake." She handed her a small bag. "And here's your prize."

"You didn't have to give me a prize but thank you." Lindsay pulled a small book out of the tissue paper and read, *Daily Devotions for the Christian Woman*. She smiled at Jenna. "I love this."

"That's *gut*. I remembered you liked reading daily prayers and inspirational messages in the morning." Jenna laughed. "Of course, if you hadn't won, I would've still given it to you."

"You're such a thoughtful person. I've been thinking about Isabella. She could stay with us. That way she'll be out of Millersburg and can keep her pregnancy a secret. The cover story can still be that she is reminded too much of Justin and needs to get away. Also, she can say that I offered her a job to help with household chores. She isn't going to Michigan now, is she?"

Jenna, sitting by her, said, "Martha has had second thoughts about Isabella coming because she fainted. Martha lives out in a rural area and Kalamazoo gets a lot of snow in the winter."

Katie's eyes widened with surprise. "I hoped Isabella would stay with Jenna and Eli. She's been turning to Jenna for advice and support. I'd love for Eli and Jenna to adopt her baby."

Jenna frowned. "They don't like we're Old Order Amish. I can see them accepting Mom's suggestion because she isn't Amish at all. It doesn't make sense but that is what it is."

"I remember a few attended our school with me and Sarah." Eli touched his beard. "They pretty much stayed by themselves during lunch."

"It might be better because she'll see how much work it is with a newborn. She'll be more eager to have her baby adopted." Lindsay took a sip of her coffee.

Harris returned to his seat with Lindsay's cheesecake and his plate filled with desserts. "We might have a little angel who sleeps a lot."

"Sure, we might," Lindsay said, grinning.

Eli glanced at Jenna. "We could have Isabella live with us when you have your baby."

"Isabella did mention living with us when she's in her last trimester. She doesn't feel that we aren't Amish enough like her parents think." Jenna sighed. "I want everything to work out for her."

"Go ahead and call Isabella tomorrow. Even if her parents should agree to her living with us, Isabella might not want to. Katie's right that she has bonded with you." Lindsay glanced at Jenna. "She doesn't know me very well. I'm anxious to learn if living with us might be a solution for them. If possible, we could go tomorrow afternoon to see Isabella." She knew Jenna had bought a cell phone for Isabella to use but she didn't want to broadcast it in front of Roman and Katie. They might not approve of Jenna buying a phone for her.

Harris nodded. "Sounds good to me. She can live with us for a few months until Lindsay has our baby, then go to Jenna's and Eli's."

"Isabella can stay with me on the weekends." Phoebe looked at Seth. "Well, until I marry this cute guy."

Seth rolled his green eyes. "Geez, for a moment, I thought you forgot about me."

"I could never forget you, but I think you forgot to tell Mom something." Phoebe raised her eyebrows at him.

He nodded. "I have your baby cradle finished."

A feeling of excitement filled Lindsay. "Thank you, Seth. I can't wait to see it."

"It's in our barn so you can see it," Jenna said. "Seth did a beautiful job."

"Would it fit in our car?" Lindsay asked.

Harris nodded. "We can try and put the back seat down."

"I can deliver it." Seth let out a long breath. "I wasn't going to mention it in case nothing came of it, but I have a job interview in Columbus."

A shadow of annoyance crossed Katie's face. "It's too bad you can't stay at your present job. I'd love for you and Phoebe to live in Millersburg."

She should be happy for her son that he has an interview, but it isn't the ideal situation. He does love the men he works with here in Millersburg, Lindsay thought. "Phoebe tried to find a job here in Millersburg, but there wasn't any position for a physician assistant. Seth, I'm sure you'll do great during the interview."

Harris took another bite of dessert. "Katie, you make the best pie. I love the flaky crust too."

Lindsay appreciated her sweet husband changing the topic away from Seth's job. She saw how relieved Phoebe looked when he did.

"Thank you." Katie looked at Lindsay. "How are you feeling?"

"I'm doing fine except I get tired."

"I'm sure it's nice carrying one baby instead of triplets," Jenna said.

Lindsay laughed. "It's a little different." She jabbed a piece of coconut cream pie off of Harris's plate.

He grinned at her. "I wondered how long you could go without taking some of my pie."

Lindsay shrugged. "I can't resist Katie's pie."

⌒

Harris crawled into bed, reaching for her, and pulling her across the mattress until she was snug against him. "How's my girl?"

"Fine, now that you're here." Being next to Harris was such a wonderful feeling and each day she gave thanks for him and their daughters. And for the new life growing inside her. Poor Isabella lost Justin because of a tragic accident. She was so young to figure out what to do and to have to face her unsympathetic parents. "I'm sorry I didn't ask you first about Isabella staying with us. I shouldn't have blurted out my plan before I talked it over with you."

"You were smart to think of it. I hope her parents are agreeable to having her move to Columbus." He kissed the top of her head. "I know you must relate to Isabella's situation. You were the same age when you were pregnant with our triplets. I wasn't there for you and Isabella doesn't have Justin. Her parents want to keep her pregnancy a secret. That puts a lot of pressure on her."

"I do feel a connection to her. I guess that's what pushes me to want to make her life easier. You'll like Isabella. I hope Jenna gets a chance to talk to her tomorrow. Or rather today. I'd rather not make the drive back to talk to them. Hopefully, it won't be too late in the afternoon. I have to get back to teach and you have to get back to work too."

"Sam's off this week so I'm taking some of his patients."
He chuckled. "Sam said they better not switch to me for
their doctor. He told me to be crabby."

"It was a surprise that he decided suddenly to take a
whole week off to go home to Wisconsin."

"I don't think it was just to see his family. He said he
reconnected with his old high school girlfriend."

"That's awesome. I'm relieved he has finally moved on
from Phoebe. Sam made her uncomfortable with his texts
and asking her out constantly."

"He made Seth unhappy too," Harris said. "For being an
intelligent guy, Sam couldn't grasp the fact that Phoebe's
taken."

She wanted to get Harris's feelings about Katie and Roman. "Did you notice how pleasant Katie was? It was nice.
I hope it goes well when Phoebe and Seth go to their house."

"Roman was laid back too. Maybe they will attend the
wedding." He kissed Lindsay on her lips. "I love you. We
better get some sleep. Tomorrow is a big day."

"I love you too. This new year will be great. We have
Phoebe's wedding to look forward to and our baby will be
born." She thought it'd be nice to have a boy this time, but
they didn't know yet. They decided to wait until the birth
because both wanted to be surprised. Although Harris had
hinted it might be nice to know ahead of time. Helen and
John had asked them if they knew if it were a boy or a girl.
She'd laughed, saying, "We only know there is one baby this
time." At a swift kicking in her belly, she laughed. "I think
baby Manning's anxious to be born. He just kicked me."

Harris laughed, placing his hand on her belly. "It's a
strong kick. I'll rub your back so you can sleep."

"You are so good to me." She murmured, her eyelids
feeling heavy. "I don't think the kicking will be an issue. I'm
tired."

Chapter Twenty

Lindsay hadn't expected Isabella's home to be depressing. The rugs were threadbare, and the bare walls needed fresh coats of paint. The stiff furniture was uncomfortable, but she understood not having extra money to spend on furnishings. After all, she'd lived in a dinky and dark apartment with her triplets before giving Amy and Jenna to Katie and Roman to raise. Then when it was just her and Phoebe, their studio apartment had been small. She had a wall bed to pull down at night.

It wasn't just the appearance, though, of the house, but something deeper. Isabella's father cast darkness in the house with his presence. Now she understood why Jenna had mentioned that Isabella had planned to live with Justin's family after marriage. From what she'd learned about Justin, he had been a warm and kind young man. It was a shame his family had moved to Pennsylvania because it seemed they were caring and kind too. If Mr. and Mrs. Glick learned about their grandchild, would they want to raise him or her? She heard Justin's father suffered from multiple sclerosis, so it wouldn't be the ideal situation for them to take the baby. She hoped Justin's parents would be happy to have the baby adopted by Jenna and Eli.

Mrs. Miller wore a brown dress. Lindsay realized she was an older version of her daughter, Isabella, except for her hair color. Her brown hair with strands of gray peeked out from beneath her white prayer *kapp*. Mr. Miller's long beard was completely white, so she guessed he was older than his wife.

As they sat in the living room, Mr. Miller said, "*Danki* for offering to have Isabella live with you." He clenched his jaw, glancing at his daughter. "Isabella has shamed us. We'd hoped she could go to Michigan, but that isn't possible now."

Mrs. Miller nodded. "It's *gut* that you have opened your home to our daughter. Isabella's a *gut* cook and can help out. If she feels ill, you can call the phone we share with our neighbor."

"We'll keep in touch to let you know about the young couple, Daniel, and Ida Troyer. They are considering adopting the baby." Mr. Miller sighed. "I wish she could've gone to stay with them now. Nothing against you but they are Amish."

Isabella's hands were folded on her lap. "I think they want to wait to see if I have a boy. I don't think that should make any difference if they want a baby to love."

He shook his head. "I never heard that is why. They want to move from Michigan to southwestern Ohio where they have some family."

Looking uncomfortable, Mrs. Miller said, "Isabella might be able to live with them the last month of her pregnancy. I'd think they would be settled in their new home by then."

Lindsay decided to speak up about what she thought might be for the best. "Isabella is welcome to stay with us the whole time. That way she won't have to move again before the baby's born."

"I wish this hadn't happened and you could stay here with us." Mrs. Miller's eyes misted over with tears, as she looked at Isabella. "I'll miss you."

"I *wish* Justin hadn't died and we'd be married." Isabella looked at her mother. "I'll miss you too. I'm sorry for all the trouble I've caused."

"Isabella can go to Columbus today with you. That way you won't have to make another trip here to get her." Mr. Miller's face had a look of determination. "If you need more time, she can take a bus in a few days."

Lindsay knew that the sooner Isabella left, the better her father would feel. It was a pity that things couldn't be different. She couldn't imagine her father telling her to leave when she was pregnant. But if he'd lived, she might not have gone to the beach in the first place. Her home wouldn't have been a place she wanted to leave. She glanced at Harris. At his nod, she said to Isabella, "Is that okay with you if you come with us this afternoon? If it isn't, we can return to get you."

"*Ya*, I can leave now, but there is something important to me. Could I take my wedding gift to your house? Justin gave me beautiful dinnerware sets a week before...the accident." She cleared her throat. "In our faith, there isn't an engagement ring given. Instead, it is customary for the groom to give a clock or a set of china to his bride."

With raised eyebrows, Mrs. Miller spoke in a rush, "You don't have to take your dishes. We'll keep them for you. Besides, Justin was generous when he gave you enough dinnerware for six people. There are a lot of boxes, so it isn't practical to take the dishes to Columbus."

Isabella rubbed her lower lip. "I could take only one or two sets with me."

"That's a nice gift from Justin," Harris said in a warm voice. "There is room in our car for your dishes."

Abigail, wearing a navy-blue dress, entered the room with a teapot. "Would you like more tea, Mrs. Manning?"

"Yes, please," Lindsay said.

After pouring tea into the cup, Abigail said, "I don't see why Isabella can't stay here."

Mr. Miller gave his daughter a harsh look. "She can't."

Isabella, rising, said, "I'll go pack my bag."

"I can help you." Mrs. Miller glanced at her husband, looking for confirmation from him.

"*Danki, Mamm,* but I can do it myself." Isabella smiled at Abigail. "You can move into my bedroom."

"*Nee,* I'm hoping you'll be coming back. It won't be the same without you here."

Lindsay ran her fingers over her skirt, smoothing a few wrinkles in it. She heard the pain in Abigail's voice. "You can write to each other and talk on the phone."

~

Isabella pulled a suitcase out from under her bed. It had been her *mammi's* and she'd hoped to use it when going somewhere with Justin. She placed it on top of her bed. Opening a drawer in her bureau, she removed underwear and night-gowns. After folding them neatly and placing them in the suitcase, she went to her armoire to get her few dresses and prayer coverings. Her winter coat was on a hook in the kitchen.

Although it was a relief not to have to go to Michigan, she felt nervous about staying with Lindsay and Harris. At least, she'd met Lindsay when they had lunch together and knew her daughters. They were such wonderful women. Her parents didn't even know she'd already met Lindsay, or that she'd paid for her doctor's visit. Would she go to a doctor in Columbus or a midwife? It was difficult to believe her parents wanted her to leave as soon as possible to live with Englishers, but they felt forced to keep her pregnancy a se-cret. Once she moved and was out of sight, they could relax a bit.

She hadn't told Molly goodbye or Jacob and Mary. Molly seemed to like to get away from them. Every chance she got to go to Jacob's, she went. *After I leave home, Molly might have to stick around here to help with chores. At least, I did see everyone during the Christmas season. I hope Mary gets pregnant soon. I know she wants a big family with Jacob.*

After Isabella set the suitcase by her door, she went to her 30-piece dinnerware set that was still in boxes in the corner of the room. The dinnerware was a complete service for six people. Sitting on the floor, she carefully lifted one box onto her lap. Removing the top plate, she admired the beautiful white plate. Tears filled her eyes, remembering how sweet Justin had been when he gave her the gift. Although she'd taken the dinnerware set to her house, they planned on moving them to his parents after the wedding. He'd given it to her the evening they attended their last singing. They were permitted to go to one more singing with their old group of friends before the wedding.

I'll take one dinnerware set with me to Columbus. It is silly to take all of them. She sighed. *I'm starting a new life in a new place and far away from my family. It'd be nice if Mamm and my sisters could take the bus to visit. I'm sure Daed won't allow that.*

She put the plate back in the box. Closing the lid, she thought about how Justin had been a part of her life for years. Sure, she was young yet, but from first grade on, he'd been there for her. She desired with her whole heart, that she'd wake up from this nightmare and he'd be alive. Instead of taking a set of her china, there was something she could easily take. It wouldn't be bulky and was precious to her too. It was hidden in an envelope under her mattress.

One evening, they'd gone with Luke and Hannah to the county fair during their *rumspringa*. Luke had used his cell phone to take photos of them. One photo was of her and Justin. Hannah had asked an English couple to take one of them together. Luke went to Walmart because he could upload them from his phone to print hard copies. She lifted the mattress enough to slide the envelope out and removed the two photos. *How happy we look*, she thought. Some nights before going to sleep, she'd looked at the photos when she needed to see Justin's face again. She opened the suitcase and put the photos on top of her clothes instead of in her purse.

It was fortunate that no one knew about the photos. They were taught that it was prideful to have photos of themselves. Their two ministers and bishop shared in their sermons how allowing pictures violated the Bible verse, Exodus 20:4: "Thou shalt not make unto thee any graven image, or any likeness of anything that is in heaven above, or that is in the earth beneath, or that is in the water under the earth."

Before leaving her room, she kneeled by her bed to pray. "Dear Heavenly Father, I am grateful for Lindsay and Harris taking me to their home. Please guide me to do right by them and to fit in. It's not just because they're Englishers, but because I'm leaving my faith. Do I ask them to take me to an Amish community so I can attend Sunday church day? Or do I go with them to their Protestant church? I don't want to be a nuisance for Lindsay and Harris, but I need your guidance in my decisions. Give me wisdom in the days ahead. In Jesus' Name, I pray."

Chapter Twenty-One

During the first couple of weeks living with Harris and Lindsay in Columbus, Isabella had been uncomfortable, but now at the end of the month, she felt like part of their family. She was used to getting up early in the morning, so she made the coffee. Lindsay only drank one cup because she didn't want to overdo the caffeine with being pregnant. It had been amazing to see a coffee maker that ground the beans first. She loved the smell of the coffee brewing. It tasted so much better than the coffee made in the metal pot on the wood stove.

Taking a hot shower daily was amazing too. She admired Lindsay for being a schoolteacher, especially for teaching math in high school. Then Harris was a doctor and all three daughters worked in the medical field. She still couldn't believe that Amy and Jenna were both EMTs. If Jenna adopted her baby, she knew he or she would benefit from being part of this successful and loving family.

As she filled the coffeepot with filtered water, Isabella looked forward to Phoebe's wedding. She'd never been to an English wedding but had gone with Lindsay and Harris to their church where Phoebe and Seth would be married. They had offered to drive her to an Amish service, but she hadn't wanted to put them out, and it wasn't like she'd known any Plain people in Columbus.

The church was beautiful with stained glass windows and rich wood carvings. She enjoyed the shorter service because their Amish service lasted close to four hours. One thing was the same thing she did at her Sunday church. They both ate after the service. Instead of the Swartzentruber Amish meal of bean soup, Lindsay, Harris, Phoebe, and Seth ate brunch at a restaurant.

She'd bought sky blue material and made a new dress to wear to the wedding. It seemed it was time to stop wearing black for mourning. Her heart was still ripped from losing Justin, but going to a wedding was a time to be happy for Phoebe and Seth.

"Good morning." Lindsay gave her a smile. "You're spoiling us. If you ever want to sleep in, I can make breakfast." She got two cups out of the cabinet and poured coffee into them.

"I wake up early and I enjoy cooking for you." She scooped out scrambled eggs from the skillet and put them on a pretty blue plate. She added bacon and toast to the plate before she did one for herself. Placing the plate on the counter, she smiled at Lindsay. "Eat up. A teacher needs her strength to deal with scholars."

Lindsay carried the cups to the granite counter. She wore a small plaid maternity top with gray pants. Her blonde hair was pulled back in a low ponytail. She definitely didn't look like a forty-something-year-old woman. Funny how they were both pregnant, yet at such different ages. "I like how you say scholars instead of students. It reminds me of Jenna's and Amy's upbringing. Well, Seth's too. They use the word scholars." Sitting on a red stool, she pointed to the one next to her. "Young lady, get off your feet and sit by me to eat."

Isabella laughed, sitting. "You sound like a teacher." She jabbed her fork into the eggs, wondering if it was wrong for her to feel comfortable in an English home. She tried to stay away from watching TV but had seen a couple of Blue Blood shows with Lindsay and Harris. At Phoebe's apartment, she'd watched a movie with her bridesmaids and Jenna. Her *mamm* had written to her that she shouldn't watch any television and to read her Bible daily. She was surprised that her father and mother had decided to have her live in Columbus with people they didn't know and certainly not their faith. They had to settle for a place far enough away from their community even though it wasn't what they thought was best for Isabella.

"Your scrambled eggs are fluffy and delicious," Lindsay said, turning her head to see Harris joining them.

He kissed Lindsay on the cheek. "I knew I better hurry and get in here before you girls ate everything."

She'd never seen her *daed* kiss her mother, but in her home, they were not demonstrative with hugs and kisses like she'd observed with Lindsay and Harris. She hoped Jenna and Eli were because it felt nice to show affection. She suspected they were affectionate even though they were Amish. Her feelings hadn't changed, and she still wanted them to adopt her baby. Her purpose in life was to give birth to a healthy baby and to hope that the right home would be Jenna's.

I'm thankful I haven't fainted again. It must've been the stress of thinking I had to go to Michigan. And telling my parents about being pregnant. I'm feeling well and I like Lindsay's obstetrician, but I miss Dr. Sullivan.

She noticed Harris helping Lindsay with her coat, realizing they'd finished eating breakfast while she'd been daydreaming. After they said goodbye, she told them to have a *gut* day.

While putting her plate in the dishwasher, the landline phone rang. She quickly picked up the receiver and saw on the caller ID, it was Hannah. She'd told her to use either the landline number or to call her cell phone. "Hi. I'm glad you called."

"Are you still doing okay?"

"*Ya*, I am doing fine. How are you and Luke?" Isabella sat on a stool, knowing conversations with Hannah were long since she'd moved away.

"He came over last evening for supper. We spent time doing a puzzle." Hannah giggled. "We went for a romantic buggy ride. It was too short, though."

She was glad Hannah felt free to talk about spending time with Luke. She wouldn't want Hannah to be afraid to share with her. It seemed like a long time ago when they were all four enjoying their lives together. "I'm glad you had a nice evening. Do you have wedding plans?"

"We talked about getting married next winter, so we're taking the kneeling vows next fall. Luke wants to save more money."

"That's wonderful. The year will go fast. You'll be a beautiful bride." Hannah had the perfect shade of green eyes, surrounded by thick eyelashes.

"What are you up to?" Hannah asked.

"I'm just cleaning up the kitchen. It's easy because Harris and Lindsay always put their plates and cups in the dishwasher before they leave for work. I finished my dress for Phoebe's wedding yesterday."

"I'm glad you decided to use blue for your dress. Sometimes I wish we weren't restricted to dark colors. You'll have to tell me all about the wedding. I doubt I'll ever go to an English wedding. The whole thing about Phoebe and Seth getting married is interesting. I mean he's marrying Phoebe and she looks like her sisters. It's crazy how he grew up with Jenna and Amy, thinking they were his sisters, then fell in love with Phoebe."

"I heard they had chemistry between them the first time they met." Isabella chuckled, loving the story of how they had first met each other. "Phoebe wore a blonde wig and glasses as a disguise when she went to the Yoders' store with her parents. She had fun teasing Seth."

"Something to hear you use the word chemistry. The smart people must be rubbing off on you."

"I doubt that."

"*Ach,* I forgot the reason I decided to call you. Tom King asked about you on Sunday. He wants to talk to you. He has it bad for you."

She let out a sigh. "I wish he'd forget about me."

"He might be the answer to your prayers. You two can marry and raise your baby together."

Isabella wished people understood that getting married was not going to happen for her. Hannah, Rebecca, and her *mamm* seemed to think that was what she should do. It didn't matter what she wanted. "*Nee,* I will never marry Tom. I don't love him, and I couldn't live in his house. It was the home Justin and I planned on sharing with his family."

"That makes sense. What should I tell him?"

"Tell Tom to find another woman to bother. He's a *wunderbaar* man, but I'm not interested in him." *Why can't Tom forget about me and find another woman to court?*

Hannah cleared her throat. "I guess you're still planning on Jenna adopting your baby."

"*Ya,* he or she will have a *gut* life with Jenna and Eli." At silence from Hannah, she said, "You can't expect me to raise my baby on my own."

"I hope you won't regret giving your baby away."

"I don't feel like I have a choice, so my adoption decision is for the best."

In a few minutes, they finished their phone conversation, but disturbing thoughts invaded Isabella's mind. She'd go to her room to rest and to pray. Once in the bedroom, she saw her blue dress for Phoebe's wedding on a hanger, draped over the top of the closet door. She thought about her wedding dress that she'd left at home. Blue was the customary color for Amish brides, and hers was a dark blue. She never wore it. It never seemed right to wear the dress when it was supposed to be for her wedding to Justin.

Sitting in a chair close to a window, she thought, *It'd been great to talk to Hannah until the mention of Tom. Hannah's voice held a hint of judgment about me giving my baby to a mature couple. Is God trying to point me in the direction of marrying Tom? Would he be persistent in pursuing me if he knew about my pregnancy? Tom's a sweet man but I don't see myself becoming his wife. I need to pray about all of this.*

"Dear Father, I thought I had it all figured out with giving my baby and Justin's to Jenna and Eli to adopt. I know that won't make my parents happy, and I should honor their wishes, but when I prayed before, I felt like You gave me the go-ahead to have Jenna be my baby's adoptive mother. Hearing about Tom's interest in me is confusing. It seems he would give up on me dating him, especially since I am not in Millersburg any longer." She took a deep breath and continued, "I'm thankful to You that Lindsay and Harris took me in to live with them. Please be with my parents and siblings during this time. Help me to have a healthy baby and prayers for Lindsay's and Harris's baby too. In Jesus' Name, I pray."

Peace washed over her and the previous stress about Tom left.

At the sound of her ringtone, she walked to the nightstand where she'd left her cell phone the previous night. She saw on the top screen that it was Jenna and quickly answered, "Hi."

"Hi. I'm at the hospital but decided to check in with you. How's life with my parents?"

"It's great." Jenna was like an older sister to her, and she liked to ask her for advice. After all, she'd been with her on the most tragic day of her life and continued to be supportive.

"I talked to Hannah today." Quickly, she told Jenna about what her friend had said about Tom. "Should I tell him I'm pregnant? I think he'll keep quiet about it, and then he can move on to a more appropriate girl."

"What if he wants to marry you because you're pregnant?" Jenna asked.

"*Nee*, I hope not. That isn't what I want. He isn't Justin and I don't want to live in Tom's house. I have many happy memories of being there with Justin and his family."

"If he continues to ask about you, maybe you should tell him. Tom was nice to drive you to the hospital to see me."

"*Ya*, I can't believe I did that. I should've waited but was anxious to find out if you'd adopt my baby."

"More than anything, I want to be a mother to your child, but I'll understand if you change your mind," Jenna said, genuine affection obvious in her voice.

"I won't change my mind. If I move in with you after my birthday, I can help you get everything ready for the baby…*your* baby. I won't dare venture to Millersburg. If someone from my community sees me in town, that wouldn't be *gut*."

"I'd love for you to live with us."

Isabella heard a man's voice, saying, "There's been an accident. We need to go."

"I have to get off here," Jenna said, a sense of urgency in her voice. "Joe said there's been an accident."

Isabella said, "I'll pray for the people to be okay. Goodbye, Jenna."

Chapter Twenty-Two

Harris kissed Phoebe's forehead as they waited to walk down the church aisle. He'd been disappointed that he hadn't gotten to walk Jenna down the aisle, but he understood that wasn't the way it was done in an Amish wedding. Even if it had been possible, he wouldn't have been the father to do it. Roman would have had the honor since he and Katie had raised Jenna. Now Amy planned on joining the Amish church. He'd thought at one time that Amy was interested in continuing her education, but she changed her mind. If she should marry, Amy would have an Amish wedding. "Phoebe, you look beautiful. You look grown up with your hair up." She wore her hair in an elegant style with a fancy hair barrette in the back.

"I am grown-up. Dad, you look handsome. I couldn't be happier today, having you walk me down the aisle to Seth." Her brown eyes filled with tears.

"We are something," he said, shaking his head. "Now, I'm tearing up. By the way, this is such a special day for me too. I'm so proud of you. Walking you to your future husband is such a wonderful thing for me." He'd tried to convince Lindsay to walk with them and that she could be on one side of Phoebe with him on the other. She decided he should do the honor without her. He thought if she hadn't been huge with their baby, she would have.

Phoebe gave a tiny laugh. "We have to stay calm. I can't ruin my makeup. I love you."

"I love you too." He saw Haley and Amy at the front smiling at them, and Emma, a school friend of Phoebe's, whispered to the flower girl and ring bearer to go next. Originally, Phoebe hadn't wanted a wedding coordinator because she hadn't thought it was necessary. However, once they changed the date, Emma offered to help. She'd left the corporate world to start her own wedding business. The young woman had been a calming influence in the short time they had to prepare for a church wedding and reception. He hoped her business would be successful. "It's going to be our turn soon. I'm glad Amy could be a bridesmaid."

Phoebe nodded. "Me too. She looks gorgeous in cranberry. I'm glad I went with cranberry and navy blue for our colors."

"Your Mom was partial to the pink you thought about having," he said, grinning.

When the music changed, Emma flashed a big smile. "Okay, it's your turn. The organist is starting your song, Phoebe. Take your time so everyone can soak in your incredible beauty."

His daughter rolled her eyes at Emma, and said, "Thank you." She exhaled a deep breath as she took his arm. "Oh my gosh, our church aisle is very long."

"It'll give me more time with you before I have to give you away."

As the wedding guests stood, then turned to look at them, Phoebe said, "There are many people here."

He thought about teasing her that he realized it was going to be a large size wedding and reception because of the money he'd paid for the dinner. He didn't mind at all paying for four hundred guests and wanted to make Phoebe's day as exceptional as she was to him. Amish weddings could easily have as many guests. Three hundred guests had attended Jenna's and Eli's wedding. Seth wanted Amish homemade noodles included with the other food items. His relatives were in charge of making enough noodles for the wedding dinner. He'd requested pies, too, even though a wedding cake would be served.

As they did their father-daughter procession, he saw smiling faces staring at them. In the front on the groom's side, Roman and Katie smiled at them. It was a relief when Phoebe and Seth learned they decided to attend the wedding. Even Katie's parents, Naomi and Clarence Gingerich came. A few of the aunts and uncles were in attendance too. Roman's parents were no longer living, but his aunt and her husband came from Florida. Jenna and Eli were seated in the front pew with Lindsay and Isabella. His parents were seated there too.

When he was close to Lindsay, Harris saw Lindsay wiping tears from her sapphire blue eyes. Suddenly, he stood in front of the minister and Seth. Harris swallowed hard when the minister asked, "Who gives this woman to be married to this man?"

He answered, "Her mother and I do." Before he stepped away to sit with Lindsay, Harris saw the tenderness in Seth's eyes and his joyful smile. *Phoebe chose well,* he thought.

⁓

At the wedding table, Seth and Phoebe gazed into each other's eyes. "Mrs. Yoder, do you think we should start visiting each table?" They decided against a receiving line but wanted to try to talk to as many guests as possible. There were ten people seated at each round table, so it wouldn't be an easy task with forty tables.

"Oh, you're so formal, Mr. Yoder, but I love hearing my new last name," Phoebe said, grinning. "Let's wait a few minutes. You haven't finished your noodles. I better learn how to make them. I doubt we can get to each table, so we can cut out my grandparents' friends if we run out of time. We'll be sure to thank everyone for coming before the end of the reception. We can have Emma get everyone's attention."

"We can start visiting after the toasts. I'm too excited to eat much, plus you're so beautiful in your dress, I can't concentrate on eating."

Phoebe nodded. "That's right. We should wait until after the toasts."

"I love your dress," Haley said. "The lace is lovely, and the pearl and crystal beading are perfect on the bodice part."

Scott gave a mischievous smile. "Seth, good luck with the tiny buttons on the back."

Why is Scott looking at my wife's back? "I'm sure I can handle it, but thanks," Seth said drily, casting him a look as he leaned forward.

Emma touched Haley's shoulder and said, "It's time to do the toasts. You go first, then Corey goes next."

Seth noticed that most of the guests already had glasses of wine for the toasts. Some Amish didn't object to having an occasional glass of wine. He thought it interesting how they had worked out the details so well for their wedding. Many English traditions were cut from their day. Phoebe wouldn't be doing a father-daughter dance and they wouldn't do a wedding dance. Because the Amish didn't believe in dancing, Phoebe suggested they should eliminate it from their reception. Although she'd teased that not doing the popular chicken dance would be missed.

Without music at the reception, there hadn't been a need for a disc jockey, so Emma filled in to make announcements when needed.

He whispered to Phoebe, "Sorry you won't get to do a father-daughter dance."

She squeezed his hand. "Dad walked me down the aisle, so that was what I wanted. The dance isn't important to me."

"We're going to do toasts to the bride and groom now." Emma handed the microphone to Haley. Then she took her seat, sitting at a nearby round table.

Haley, rising, faced the guests with a smile. She wore her blonde hair up, so it would look similar to Amy's black hair being done in a bun and not worn down. She wore a silver necklace that Phoebe had given Haley for being her matron of honor. She hesitated in giving Amy a necklace. When her mom had married, she didn't get any jewelry for the bridesmaids to wear because Amish women never wear any. However, Amy said she'd like a necklace too. She wasn't baptized yet she'd explained, and the jewelry would be something she could keep to remember the special day.

"I'm Haley Crawford and I'm happy to be Phoebe's matron of honor. First, I want to thank Seth's family and Phoebe's for the delicious food. Your families know how to serve a wonderful wedding meal. I love how you combined favorite dishes from both sides of your families. I've known Phoebe my whole life. She's not only a close friend but is like a sister to me. Whenever we happened to be in the same classes, the teachers quickly separated us from sitting next to each other. We couldn't be quiet. We've done many things together, but running together in the morning is special to us. We talk about what is important to us. Of course, I'm the better runner."

She laughed, glancing at Phoebe. "Just kidding. Many of our conversations have involved Seth and how Phoebe couldn't imagine life without him. I love how she met him at his parents' store in Millersburg. She teased Seth in the store, and they connected instantly. They faced a big challenge with their very different upbringings, but their love has been strong enough to get to this point…their wedding day."

Haley turned to look at Seth and Phoebe. "I know your hearts will continue to seek the Lord in your decisions as a married couple." She raised her wine glass. "Congratulations to Phoebe and Seth. I wish you both the best of luck on this amazing journey that is being husband and wife. To marriage!"

After Haley returned to her seat, Phoebe whispered, "Thank you. You're the best friend ever."

⁓

Seth watched as Corey stood, grateful that he'd agreed to be his best man.

"I'm Corey Lung and I'm honored to be Seth's best man. I've known him for several years from our construction jobs. When I showed up for my new job on the building site, I met Seth for the first time. I was nervous but he told me that the crew and foreman were great. He gave me the confidence I needed to be able to do good work. By lunchtime, I realized I had left my lunch back at the business site. We all traveled in a van to where we were supposed to work. There wasn't any restaurant close by that I could walk to. When I told Seth my dilemma, he looked at his lunch for a long moment, then said, "Here, I'll share mine with you. I have plenty."

Corey chuckled as he glanced at the guests. "Now, most of you probably know that Seth has a big appetite, so sharing his lunch was generous." He paused for a moment. "As a couple, Phoebe and Seth, are wonderful together. I've enjoyed spending time with them. They both have a great sense of humor, but Phoebe's jokes are funnier." He smiled at Phoebe as Seth shrugged and flashed a grin.

Corey continued, "Their love for each other is genuinely inspiring. I saw the radiance and happiness shining on their faces again today. May God continue to bless you in your marriage." Corey raised his wine glass high. "Seth and Phoebe, to a lifetime of good health, love, and joy."

As Corey took his seat next to him, Seth said, "Thanks. You did a good job."

Phoebe whispered, "Roman and my dad were amazing when they welcomed everyone before we ate. Roman mentioned how happy he is to have me as a daughter-in-law. That was so great to hear."

Seth hated to tell Phoebe that his parents still had hopes she'd choose to become Amish. Their reasoning was that when they had children, it would make sense to them to live a simple life and have the family grounded in the strong, Amish life. After all, Lindsay had seen the value in having them as parents to Amy and Jenna because of their lifestyle.

They decided to appear accepting to their Protestant wedding and felt eventually Seth and Phoebe would come to their senses and realize being Amish was the best thing for them. Their prayers for this to happen were a constant in their lives. His parents were being delusional but at least, they were at their wedding. Sure, he did all this work by getting his high school diploma, driver's license, and buying a car, and clothes for his new lifestyle, but they had faith he might change his mind.

Becoming English hadn't been an overnight decision. He'd prayed forever it seemed what to do. In his heart, he was where he was supposed to be for the love of his life. "Harris did a great job on the prayer." He sipped his wine. "We better get started on visiting with some of our guests before we cut the cake."

~

Seth wore the green swim trunks that Phoebe gave him as a wedding gift. She bought the trunks to match his green eyes. She wore a pink one-piece swimsuit instead of her red two-piece. She'd said, "No Christmas colors on the beach." They were holding hands while in comfortable chairs under an umbrella and soaking up the beauty of the beach. *It sure beats the cold weather we left in Ohio*, he thought. *It is going to be awesome*

*to be here for Valentine's Day too. I need to find a florist to order a
dozen roses for Phoebe.*

He loved hearing the sound of the waves as the refreshing, ocean breeze washed over him. "I can't decide what is
more beautiful. The incredible blue water, the sandy beach,
or you." He turned to stare at his wife. He loved that finally,
Phoebe was his wife. "Of course, you are the most beautiful."

"Wow, that's saying a lot that you choose me when we're
surrounded by gorgeous weather on a beach." Phoebe
leaned closer to his face and gave him a kiss. "I can't believe
we're here after that long trip. You did great flying for the
first time, especially since we had to fly so long to get to
Maui."

He laughed, remembering how she seemed nervous on
the plane when he hadn't been. "You were more restless
than me. Here, I thought you were a seasoned flier."

"You were fascinated with watching the movies on the
flights. I do get restless when I fly, but I didn't want to tell
you that and worry you about flying." She gave him an embarrassed look. "I'm glad we spent our wedding night in Columbus. And you surprised me with staying in a swanky
hotel room instead of my apartment. It was perfect."

Since they were not leaving right away after their honeymoon, he'd booked an expensive honeymoon suite. He
grinned at her. "What else was perfect?"

"The chocolate-covered strawberries were delicious." A
smile curved her lips. "Okay, smarty pants. Our lovemaking
was perfect. You were wonderful. I'd glad we moved up our
wedding date. I love being married to you. I love you."

He put his arm around her shoulders. "Me too. I love
you. We belong together."

Chapter Twenty-Three

In early March, Isabella felt sad as Lindsay and Harris finished the nursery for their baby. She couldn't do anything for her baby except make plans to give him away. She was a little jealous that Lindsay had a loving husband, a baby on the way, three beautiful daughters, and a nice home. For the first few months, Lindsay wanted their newborn in the master bedroom. She planned on breastfeeding and had already purchased nursing bras. She knew that Lindsay had it hard for years and deserved to have a happy life.

If Justin had lived, their parents would have loved having the first grandchild in both families. She did hear *gut* news that her brother and wife were in the family way. With the closeness in ages, the two babies could've played together when they got older.

Isabella had nothing ready for her baby. If Justin hadn't died, they would be getting ready for their baby together. When would the hurt go away? Even if she hadn't been pregnant, her grief would still be great. Everyone told her that time heals, but she would never forget Justin. No one could take his place in her heart.

Has Jenna started getting ready for her baby? Probably not. She could think I'll change my mind about adoption. I need to move in with

Jenna and Eli soon. I know Lindsay could use my help with her baby, but Helen plans on visiting to spend time with her new grandchild. She imagined that Harris would be a hands-on dad.

It was sweet how he catered to Lindsay all the time. Phoebe lives close so said she would help as much as possible too. I don't think they need me to stick around to help. And I want Harris and Lindsay to have time alone before the baby is born. I was shoved into moving in with them, and as much as I love being here, it's time for me to move back to Millersburg. If I move soon, I can be there for my birthday. I can invite Abigail and Hannah to Jenna's house for my birthday. I miss them. They won't tell anyone I'm living there.

While sipping her tea, another thing bothered her. Feeling the baby's movement inside her was exciting and reassuring, but that fact made her more determined to give him or her away to Jenna. It was a reminder that she needed to move to live with the future family of her child. He was a real person needing a safe and stable home when he came into this world. She had nothing to give an infant except her love but how could that be enough?

She put her cup down and drummed her fingers against the granite countertop. Glancing at the clock, she saw it was four o'clock, and Lindsay would be home soon. She didn't need to worry about cooking supper because it was Friday. Harris brought home pizza and salads for them each Friday. *I'll call Jenna now and if she doesn't answer, I'll leave a message for her to call me.*

She heard Jenna's breathless voice say, "Hi, Isabella. I'm glad you called."

"Did I get you at a bad time? Are you home?"

"*Ya,* I just got home from work."

"Do you have a few minutes?" Isabella asked. "I need to ask you something."

"Of course, I have time for you. I hope you're feeling okay."

"I'm fine. I love staying with your parents, but what do you think of me moving to your house soon?" She decided to get to the reason for her call quickly. "I can always return for a few days when Lindsay has her baby to help out."

"I'd love for you to live with us now. You can see Dr. Sullivan again. I think that will be better too. We can wait and see how long Grandma Helen stays. She says she'll help for a week, but I can see her staying longer. Dad plans on taking time off from work to be with the baby and Mom." Jenna laughed. "It'll be more peaceful here, that's for sure."

"Harris will be a big help. He loves Lindsay so much." For a brief moment, she thought about how Justin would've taken good care of her. He had been a sweet, caring, and loving man.

"The only disadvantage I can think of is your parents won't like you living with us."

"They'll have to accept my decision. I want to help you get ready for your baby. I still want you and Eli to be his parents."

"We want your baby. He or she will be loved, but you still have time to decide what to do. I don't want you to regret later that we're raising your baby."

Isabella cleared her throat. "It'll be hard, but I feel it is the best and right thing to do. I feel God wants this for my baby."

"Eli is outside in the barn taking care of our horse, but I'm sure he'll be happy to have you move in with us now. Hey, your birthday is coming up."

"I'll be eighteen in two weeks. I'm hoping Abigail and Hannah will come to see me on my birthday. They won't mention to anyone I'm back in Millersburg. I don't want my parents to know right away that I'm back."

"That's another good reason for you to move, so you can see Abigail and Hannah, but you won't be as free to go places."

Isabella exhaled a deep breath. "It'll be hard to stay out of town. I've enjoyed shopping and going to restaurants with Lindsay and Harris."

"You can go to church with us because I've never seen anyone from your district attend our services. It's sad how they feel like avoiding us is essential."

"I know, yet we were allowed to attend your Amish school. I'll make new *kapps* that look like yours." She didn't want someone to notice she wore a Swartzentruber prayer covering. She needed to fit in when attending church with Jenna and Eli. It might be a bad idea to go to church with being pregnant. Questions would be asked about where she came from and where her *ehemann* was. Or they might not realize she was pregnant. She wasn't showing much yet, especially in her loose Amish clothing. Also, wearing an apron over her dress hid her pregnancy.

"I can see if Seth and Phoebe could bring you to my house."

"I can take a bus and get as close as I can to town. Maybe I can hire a driver to go the rest of the way." She hated for the newlyweds to have to drive her.

"No, you don't need to take a bus. I'm sure Mom and Dad can bring you if Phoebe can't. Seth does have unfinished furniture in the barn that he can work on."

"*Danki.* I'll talk to your parents tonight." Isabella heard the garage door opening. "I'm excited about living with you guys. *Danki* so much. I better get off here."

"I'm thrilled too. We'll talk again soon. Bye."

⌣

Isabella said, "I love pizza night." They were seated on the chairs by the table. Harris put all the food and drinks on the table instead of the counter.

"I do too." Lindsay took another piece out of the box. "I miss not being able to eat the pizza with everything on it. The spicy sausage gives me heartburn." She raised her eyebrows at Isabella, eyeing her piece with all the toppings. "I noticed you don't seem to have this problem. Lucky you."

"Maybe it's because she's not as far as long as you. Don't forget to eat your salads, girls."

Lindsay said, grinning, "Okay, Dad."

"It's hard to believe how I couldn't tolerate food in January, now I can eat everything. Thanks, Harris, for getting the pizza and salads." *Should I mention my conversation with Jenna while we're eating?*

"I'm glad you enjoy eating again." Lindsay asked, "Have you heard from your parents or your siblings?"

She nodded. "I received a letter from Abigail today. She saw Tom King last Sunday, but he didn't ask about me. That's a relief. And she wrote that *Mamm* is sad a lot."

"I'm sure your mother and family miss you. Before you know it, you'll be back home," Lindsay said.

"Well, that's the plan but I'm never sure about my *daed*. I talked to Jenna today about moving back to Millersburg. She said I could live with them." In a rush, she continued, "I'll come back to help you when your baby's born, but I'd like to go back to see Dr. Sullivan and help Jenna get ready for my baby. I still want her and Eli to adopt my baby."

Lindsay pushed a lock of her blonde hair behind her ear, looking at her. "That makes sense for you to live with Jenna, but I'll miss you. You've become like a daughter to me."

"I'll miss you too. I've loved living here."

Harris frowned. "I hate to see you go too. You're always welcome here."

"That's good to know." She smiled at Harris and Lindsay. "I might be back."

As they finished eating, Isabella picked through the memories from the last several months and thought about all the things she'd gone through. Even though she'd lost Justin, she faced the changes she needed to make to survive. It was never easy, especially with recurring dreams of the buggy accident. Then the memory of her parents trying to ship her off to Michigan to a stranger's house. The stress and not being to eat must have caused her to faint. Going back to the same hospital where Justin had died, had made her sad.

Was she doing the right thing to go to Jenna's? She liked Dr. Sullivan a lot but her baby would be born at the same hospital. At least, a birth should be a happy time and replace the memory of death.

What should I do after the baby is born? Is it possible for me to return home after living with an Old Order Amish family and giving their grandchild to them to adopt?

Her parents and their district felt they held on to the true Amish ways while the Old Order was open to technology and acceptance of things that were not Amish and conservative enough.

Will my parents ever forgive me? Will I be able to adjust to living the simple life as a Swartzentruber Amish woman? I don't see why my Amish district is opposed to indoor plumbing and many other things. I don't miss cooking on a wood stove and I like sleeping in a warm bedroom on a cold winter night. Jenna's house has many of the same things I like now, but no electricity. I can live without electricity, but I'm not sure I can go back to the way my family lives.

If I can't return to live with my family, it'd be great to visit Rebecca and Abe in Lancaster. I could get a job and find a place to live there. Well, that is a farfetched idea but I have to figure out something to do once I'm no longer pregnant.

When the landline rang, Harris went to the kitchen to answer it. "Hi, Jenna. Yes, we heard. We haven't talked about when Isabella will leave. If it's okay with Lindsay and she feels okay, I can drive Isabella to your house whenever she wants to go."

Lindsay nodded. "I want to go. I'd like to see Jenna and Amy. We could spend tomorrow night at Jenna's."

Harris raised an eyebrow. "Are you sure you can make the trip? You've been tired and have had pelvic pain. You should ask your doctor since you're at eight months."

"I can take a bus," Isabella said, feeling terrible that she talked about moving now. She hadn't thought about it being hard on Lindsay to make the trip.

"I should be fine. The pelvic pain is normal and just from the baby growing. We can go tomorrow."

Harris shrugged. "I guess you heard. We'll see you tomorrow." After a pause, he continued, "Brunch sounds great. Okay, she's right here." He walked to the table with the cordless phone, handing it to Isabella. Then he gathered up their empty paper plates and threw them in the trash can.

"Hi." Isabella giggled. "I guess you must be anxious for me to live with you guys."

Jenna gave a little laugh. "You're right! I'm off this weekend so you can come tomorrow. Mom and Dad can spend Saturday night before making the trip home. Does that sound okay?"

"*Ya*. I don't have much to pack, so tomorrow is fine for me."

Chapter Twenty-Four

Jenna fluffed the extra throw pillows on the queen-size bed with the quilt covering it. It had been a wedding gift from her *mammi* and was beautiful. She glanced around the bedroom to see if she'd missed anything. The blue curtains looked pretty against the pale blue wall. She liked the chair and small desk against one wall. Her English grandparents had given her both plus the beautiful armoire. *I hope Isabella will like living here and will still want me to adopt her baby. I wonder if she'll have a boy or a girl.*

"Everything is fine. Isabella will like having this room." Eli pulled her into his arms, brushing his lips against hers. "I love seeing your hair down."

Her black hair was down her back to below her waist. She felt his fingers ruffle through her hair. After kissing him, she tasted blueberry muffins. Eli could never resist her muffins. "It's freeing to have it out of the bun." Sighing, she said, "I'm nervous about Isabella feeling comfortable here. She talked about coming here after she turned eighteen, but I thought it'd be a couple of months from now. Well, I guess she'll be in her last trimester soon. She did mention moving here sometime during her last three months."

"I'm glad she's decided to come today."

"I don't want to do or say anything that might cause Isabella to decide not to have us adopt her baby."

"You won't cause her to change her mind. If she does, we can handle it together."

She smiled. "Two pregnant women in the house could've been a little much for Dad. I'm kidding. He hasn't said anything. I hope Mom can handle the road trip. Phoebe's working on Saturday."

He arched his eyebrow. "Has your mom been sick?"

"No, but she's been tired and is eight months pregnant."

"Did you get a chance to tell Amy they're coming today?"

"*Ya*, I did. She's bringing an egg, sausage, and cheese casserole for our brunch. And I made a fruit salad, muffins, and coffeecake." When she kissed his lips, he crushed her against him in a fierce embrace. When they broke apart, Jenna said, "You always make everything better."

"Hello. Anyone home? I knocked on the door before I came in."

"We're upstairs, Amy. We'll be right down," Jenna yelled back to her sister, then said in a softer voice for Eli's benefit, "More kissing later."

"You promise?"

"*Ya*, I promise."

With Eli right behind her on the stairs, they went straight to the kitchen. Jenna saw the casserole on the counter and noticed her sister wore a lavender dress. "Sweet, we're both wearing lavender. I wonder if Dad will be able to tell us apart." It was a joke that their dad couldn't at times tell them apart, especially if they were in the same room. Their mom never had this problem, and it was amazing since she hadn't raised them.

"I understand now why you two weren't around to greet me. Are you forgetting something?" Amy flashed her a smile.

Jenna ran her fingers through her hair. "*Ach*, I was busy getting Isabella's room ready. I forgot to do my hair and put a *kapp* on."

"Sure, we'll go with that. Is that your story too, Eli?"

He nodded. "I always agree with my beautiful *fraa*."

"*Danki,* for bringing the casserole. I'll hurry and do my hair. I don't want Isabella to see me without my hair covered." Smiling, she said, "I need to appear presentable."

Fifteen minutes later, her parents and Isabella arrived. Jenna took Isabella upstairs to show the bedroom to her. "It's a *wunderbaar-gut* room, Jenna. I feel blessed to have you make room for me. And your parents were kind to have me live with them."

"We're happy to have you here. I want to have a birthday party for you, but we can talk more about that later."

"I don't want you to go to any trouble. I only want to invite Abigail and Hannah."

"I'll show you the bathroom. It's across the hallway. There is natural lighting in the bathroom with that high window."

Isabella stared for a moment at the shower and sink. "I love the gray walls and the shower is such a nice size. It's *wunderbaar* seeing the outdoors from the window. Your house is gorgeous."

"*Danki.* We didn't make any changes to it really, so Eli was happy. He'd said it cost enough and good we didn't have to spend money on changing anything. They left the appliances so that was huge too. We were surprised at everything the previous Amish family thought of when they'd built this house." Isabella wore a blue dress similar to the one she wore to the wedding.

She liked seeing her in more colorful dresses instead of the black clothing she'd been wearing. *Does this mean Isabella is trying to move on with her life? Since the women in their Amish district are only allowed to wear darker colors, Isabella won't be able to continue to wear the pretty blue dresses,* Jenna thought. "I can show you the rest of the house later. We better go downstairs and eat before the food gets cold."

Isabella smiled. "Everything smells so *gut*. I smell cinnamon."

"That's from the coffee cake I made. You'll love Amy's casserole."

As they joined the others in the kitchen, Jenna handed a plate to Isabella. Amy had put the hot food on the counter to make it easier instead of putting everything on the table to be passed around which was the Amish way of serving.

Her mom was seated at the table with only a small portion of casserole and one muffin. "Mom, aren't you hungry?"

"I thought I'd start small. Everything looks delicious."

With filled plates, Jenna sat by Eli while Isabella took a chair by Amy. Eli said, "Let's pray. Dear Father, Thank You for putting us together as a family, and thank You for this food. May the meal nourish our bodies so that we have the energy to accomplish our purposes in this world. We thank you for all of the gifts you've given to those around this table. In Jesus' Name, we pray. Amen."

Although Amish prayed silently at mealtimes, Jenna appreciated Eli praying out loud. When non-Amish asked about their silent prayers, it was explained the Lord's Prayer was said. When the man of the house cleared his throat, that was the signal it was time to eat.

After they raised their bowed heads, Harris jabbed his fork into the casserole. "Thank you for fixing this brunch."

Jenna smiled. "It worked out so well since we have today off."

"I helped out by sampling the muffins before you arrived," Eli said, grinning.

Amy shook her head. "We used to accuse Seth of *sampling* our desserts before they got to the table."

"My *bruder* has a sweet tooth, that's for sure," Isabella said.

"I'm thankful it's a weekend. I'm looking forward to next month. I'll quit teaching when spring break starts." Lindsay sipped her water. "The school has hired a substitute for my classes."

Harris swallowed a bite of food. "I'll be glad when you aren't teaching and have a couple of weeks to rest before our baby is born."

Amy nodded. "That'll be nice for you to stay home. I wish you would've allowed us to have a baby shower for you. We still can if you change your mind. And you know it's a boy, so it'll be fun to choose things for him."

Lindsay patted Harris's arm. "Someone couldn't wait to be surprised, but it's nice to know ahead."

Harris laughed. "That's not the way I remember it. You were getting anxious to find out."

She rolled her eyes at him. "Helen has already bought a lot of baby items for us, but that's sweet you girls offered to have a shower for me."

Jenna thought of another reason that her mother hadn't wanted them to throw her a shower. She might have considered how Isabella would feel when she wouldn't have a baby shower. Jenna couldn't think of a way to include her in the baby conversation. It was uncomfortable because she wasn't planning on keeping her baby. Looking at Isabella, she said, "I remember you said you haven't been to my parents' store in town. I'll take you some time. I've never seen any of your family there or any Swartzentruber Amish. It should be safe."

"I'd like that."

"Katie and Roman have everything you could want in their store," Eli said.

Harris nodded. "It's a great store."

Amy chuckled. "I recall on your first visit, you and Mom bought so much that I had to order more items."

For the rest of the meal, they continued talking about the store and how Katie and Roman enjoyed being the owners.

Lindsay put her plate and glass by the kitchen sink. "After I help clean up, I'd like to go home instead of spending the night." She looked at Harris. "Is that okay with you if we go home today?"

"Sure, we can leave this afternoon, but you must not be feeling well. Is there anything I can do for you before we leave?"

"Since we've been here, I've been having Braxton Hicks contractions."

Isabella looked worried, as she stepped away from the table. "What does that mean? Are you going to have the baby earlier than your due date?"

Lindsay shook her head. "They're false contractions and aren't painful. I'm just uncomfortable and feel weird. If I change positions, they go away."

"Sit down and rest. Or you can go to our bedroom." Jenna put her arm around Lindsay's shoulders, thinking her mom's belly looked huge in her maternity jeans and top. *She has popped out a lot since the wedding.*

"I'm okay but thanks. I just feel it's a good idea for us to go home." She took a shallow breath.

"Are you having trouble breathing?" Jenna frowned.

"Yes, but the shortness of breath happens during pregnancy. Isabella has experienced it too."

Isabella nodded. "I have had shortness of breath. Lindsay, I'm sorry you had to make the trip. I could've waited to leave until it was a *gut* time for Phoebe and Seth to drive me here."

"I wanted to make the trip and am glad we did. I haven't seen my daughters and Eli since Phoebe and Seth's wedding. I'm going to use the bathroom." Lindsay laughed. "Another fun thing about being pregnant is going to the bathroom frequently."

After she left the room, Harris said, "Phoebe had to work today. It was her turn to take a Saturday. She offered to bring Isabella tomorrow, but Lindsay and I wanted to make the trip. I wonder if Lindsay has a bad headache too. She's been getting a lot of headaches."

"When you get home, be sure to call us." Jenna blamed herself for asking her parents to bring Isabella. *It wasn't urgent for Isabella to come today. I should've been thinking about Mom and not even asked them to make the trip. Mom doesn't seem like herself today. She's having trouble breathing. But that is normal when the baby gets larger and presses on the abdomen. There isn't much room now. When Isabella decides she wants something, she can't wait. Just like when she asked Tom to take her to the hospital to see me about adoption. She had months left of her pregnancy.*

Amy said, "Let's get busy on the dishes, so Mom won't try to do them." She poured dish detergent into the sink and turned on the hot water faucet.

"That's a *gut* idea." Jenna picked up the other plates except for Eli's coffee cup. He hadn't finished his second cup.

"I can help," Isabella said.

"I'll give you a dishrag to wipe off the table." Jenna smiled at the young woman. "I'm glad you're here."

Sighing, Isabella said, "I hope Lindsay will be okay on the trip back."

As he walked back into the kitchen, Harris said, "We're going to head back to Columbus."

Lindsay wasn't far behind Harris. "Sorry, we can't stay longer." She hugged Amy and Jenna and laughed, moving her hand to her belly. "Did you feel that kick? Your little brother's kicking."

"I did," Amy and Jenna said in unison.

After Harris helped Lindsay with her jean jacket, he hugged their daughters.

Lindsay hugged Isabella and said, "Thanks for everything you did for us. Keep us updated about your doctor visits. We'll miss you."

With tears in her eyes, Isabella said, "You guys are the best. I'll miss you too."

Harris said, "Take care of yourself."

Chapter Twenty-Five

Lindsay put her head against the car headrest, relieved that Harris was driving them back to Columbus. "I was afraid to mention that I was spotting in front of Jenna and Amy. I didn't want to make a big deal about it, and I didn't want to make Isabella more uncomfortable."

"I'm glad you called your OB." Harris turned his head away from the road to look at her. "I'll drive you to your appointment on Monday. You should stay home from school on Monday."

"I'm not bleeding, only some spotting, but if things change, I won't teach on Monday."

"We can order take-out tonight and you need to rest."

"I am hungry now. I should've grabbed a muffin to take with me."

"We can go through the drive-through and get you the parfait yogurt you like at McDonald's."

She lifted her head. "I can wait until we're at home. If I stay home with our baby the first few years instead of returning to teaching, will you be disappointed that you gave up your practice in Cincinnati?"

"No, are you kidding? It's wonderful living close to Phoebe. I like my practice here too. I never have regretted moving." Harris took his right hand off the steering wheel and squeezed her hand. "If you want to quit teaching to take care of our baby, that's fine with me."

Her cell phone rang with a call from Phoebe. She lifted it out of the cup holder. "Hi, Phoebe."

"Mom, I heard you and Dad left early from Jenna's. Are you okay?"

Lindsay hated hearing the concern in Phoebe's voice. "I'm fine but I wasn't feeling well and decided I didn't want to climb the stairs to sleep. I'm thankful we have a ranch."

"Tell her about the spotting," Harris said.

"I heard what Dad said. Did you call your OB?"

"I did. If I have more spotting or bleeding, I'll call her, but I have an appointment on Monday."

"Seth and I should've taken Isabella to Millersburg. Isabella could've waited. I can tell she's a teenager and can't wait when she decides to do anything."

"I wanted to see Amy and Jenna. Even though we weren't there long, it was good to visit with them."

"Maybe you should quit teaching now instead of waiting until next month."

"I'll see what my OB says on Monday."

"I have to go. I have another patient to see before I leave today. I love you and Dad. We can talk more later when you get home."

"We love you too. Bye." Lindsay blew out a deep breath as the call ended. She saw Harris turn into the McDonald's parking lot. "Nice they have their restaurants close to the highways."

"Do you want to use the restroom?"

"No, you can order from the drive-through window."

In a few minutes, she was dipping the plastic spoon into her yogurt, and they were back on the road. "You should have gotten a snack to eat."

"I ate a lot at Jenna's." He paused for a moment. "You didn't mention the stairs."

"I didn't think of it until we got there. I shouldn't use the stairs since I only have a month left. I thought about sleeping in a chair, but Jenna would've insisted that we sleep in their bedroom on the first floor." She did have a flight of stairs in her apartment when she had been pregnant with the triplets, but she wouldn't mention that to Harris. He'd feel guilty again that he hadn't been part of her life then.

Grinning, he said, "I could've carried you up to the bedroom."

She laughed. "I know you're strong, but I wouldn't want you to do that." She ate another spoonful of yogurt and wondered why Isabella decided to move to Jenna's so quickly. "I hope I didn't say something to offend Isabella."

"We're making good time and should be home in forty-five minutes." He turned his face to look at her. "I don't know why she decided to suddenly leave. We haven't watched a lot of TV. I know her faith forbids that."

She disagreed. Harris had watched a lot of college football and professional football. "It could be she felt we should have time alone without her around, but we enjoyed including her in everything we did." Wiping her lips with a napkin, Lindsay continued, "Or it was hard for her to see us as a couple having a child when she'd have the baby without Justin. She did talk before about going to Jenna's later when it was closer to her delivery."

"Her parents might not like her there, but it makes more sense to me to have her live with an Amish couple than us. I don't get why Isabella's church doesn't care for the Old Order Amish."

She nodded. "It is strange." As she gazed at Harris, she noticed he had stubble on his jaw. She loved his black hair and brown eyes. Her husband was a handsome guy, and he took excellent care of her. Each day she gave thanks to God for him. "I hope our son looks like you. We should get busy and pick out names for him."

"I prefer he has your beautiful blue eyes."

"How about Alfred or Leonard? Both names go well with Manning." She rubbed her chin. "Or Ralph is a good name."

"I know you're teasing me." After a brief silence, he said, "How about William, for your dad?"

She wiped tears from her eyes. "My dad was the best. I like you suggested his name for our baby." She squeezed his broad shoulder. "Thank you."

⌣

Three weeks later, Lindsay delivered a healthy baby, weighing eight pounds and two ounces. Their baby was in her arms. Harris sat on a chair next to her hospital bed. Strong emotions swept through him at the sight of mother and infant. "I'm proud of you. You did a great job. I love you, Lindsay." He blinked away the tears in his eyes as he gazed at her.

"You did great yourself, Dad. I'm glad you got to cut the cord."

He nodded. "It's good you didn't need a C-section this time and got to nurse him right away."

"Congratulations, Mom and Dad. He's a beautiful baby," Dr. Jeannie Avery said. "And a long baby at twenty-two inches."

Lindsay laughed. "I can believe that. He took up a lot of room. It seemed like he was right below my ribs with his kicks and also low in my abdomen the last month or so. Thank you for delivering him."

Dr. Avery said, "It was my pleasure. I'll check on you tomorrow morning." She smiled as Phoebe walked into the room, carrying a vase of six yellow roses and a stuffed bear. "I see you're back to see your brother. I have a feeling this will be a popular room."

Dr. Avery knew that Lindsay had called her daughters when she started labor early on Monday morning, but only Phoebe could make it to join them in the birthing room.

Jenna and Amy planned on coming when they finished their early shift at work. They had a driver lined up to make the two-hour trip.

"I have to see my brother again before I go to work. William's so adorable. I love you named him after your dad and the middle name is Harris." She put the flowers and toy on the hospital tray. "Flowers for the mother and one gift for the baby." Phoebe removed a box from her big purse. "And a box of chocolates for the father."

"Thank you. How did you do this so quickly?" Lindsay asked.

"I know people."

"I guess you do," Lindsay said. "I'm going to the bathroom if you want to hold him."

"I was hoping I could." Phoebe squirted sanitizer on her hands, and after rubbing it in, she took William in her arms. She sat on a blue loveseat and kissed William on the top of his head.

Harris got up from his seat and helped Lindsay from the bed. "I'll be your escort to the bathroom. I don't want you to fall."

Pointing to her hospital socks, she said, "I should be fine with these on my feet, but I love having such a good-looking escort."

When Harris returned to his chair, Phoebe asked, "Are Grandma and Grandpa coming today?"

"They left Cincinnati a few minutes ago. The way my dad drives, they'll make great time. Unless he gets pulled over for speeding." Harris smiled. "This is such a wonderful day and you being a part of it makes it even more special."

"Aww, Dad, you're a sweetheart. I'm happy you and Mom made me a big sister to this cutie pie." She looked at her brother with tenderness in her eyes. "I wonder if he'll keep his dark hair. I heard babies lose their hair in the early weeks and the hair comes in a different color."

With Harris's help, Lindsay got back in bed, pulling the sheet over her legs. "He might not. You and your sisters never lost your baby hair, and it stayed black. I'm glad I got to breastfeed him right after delivery. William likes to nurse and that reminds me of you as a baby."

Although he was happy that his parents were in a hurry to see William, Harris hoped they would just stay one night. When Lindsay and the baby were discharged, he planned on staying home for three weeks. His partners had approved of his paternity leave and understood how important it was to him. He'd missed out by not being around when their triplets were born, and he planned on enjoying every minute with Lindsay and William.

In a way, it was nice Isabella had decided to go to Jenna's before William was born. His mother wanted to visit after he went back to work to do laundry and fix meals for them, so she could get her grandmother time in then.

"You should take a nap before my parents get here. You have to be tired."

She yawned. "I am exhausted."

"I need to leave soon," Phoebe said. "I called and said I'd be a few minutes late to work."

"I'll take the baby and see if he wants to nurse, then I'll take a nap."

Before leaving the room, Phoebe said, "I told Grandma and Grandpa to stay overnight at my apartment."

"That's good because I'm going to spend the night here."

"Harris, you don't need to do that," Lindsay protested. "You won't get enough sleep."

"I can sleep anywhere." He opened his box of chocolates and grinned at the two women. "Don't worry. I'll share my candy."

"You can share with Mom. I don't want any."

After Phoebe left, Lindsay pulled her gown down and nursed William. Her blonde hair touched her shoulders, and she had a sweet expression of love as she looked at William.

She is beautiful nursing our baby, he thought. *Sometime soon I need to order flowers. I doubt Lindsay will be here long. I'll call a florist when Mom and Dad are here.* A couple of weeks ago, he bought a white gold necklace with Mom engraved on one side and William engraved on the other side. It was at home, but he could have Phoebe and Seth stop and get it for him.

Lindsay had done such a great job at having an unmedicated labor. He knew her pregnancy hadn't been easy at her older age, but she'd done well with doing everything that was needed to do to stay healthy.

Chapter Twenty-Six

Isabella wrapped the birdhouse for the young English woman. It was the last birdhouse they had for sale. I wonder if Seth has time to make more birdhouses for his parents' store. They were a popular item. He's busy with his new construction job in Columbus. However, he talked about how he might take Harris up on using space in their basement to make his wood furniture and birdhouses.

"My grandfather will love this for his birthday. He enjoys sitting outside in his wheelchair in warm weather. This is a wonderful store. I'll be back before we leave Millersburg. I want to check with my husband to see if I can buy the quilt. My name is Lynne and I'll call if I can't make it back to get it."

Her auburn, curly hair was chin length and swung forward as she spoke. She wore jeans with holes in the knees and a pink blouse. It was curious to see Englishers wearing torn jeans in town. Some were tourists, like this young customer. Jenna said they bought their jeans with holes in them. She couldn't understand why anyone would pay good money for ripped clothing.

"I can try to save the quilt for you for a few days and put sold on it." Isabella saw Katie stop straightening items on the shelves by the front door. "Katie, is that okay?"

"*Ya*, if someone else comes in and wants to buy the quilt, we can call you first." Katie smiled at Lynne. "It is a beautiful quilt. My friend Miriam made it."

"Thank you so much." Lynne ran a finger over her lower lip. "I might have to bring my husband in to see it. I want to buy it for our bed. I love the different shades of blue against the white background."

Isabella handed the birdhouse to Lynne. "Thank you. I hope you can get the quilt. Have a great day."

After Katie opened the door for Lynne, she returned to where Isabella stood behind the cash register. "You're doing such a great job."

Isabella said, "I love working here. I'm glad you gave me this job." *I won't mention that my parents will disown me for sure and certain if they learn I'm working in a store. And I shouldn't be in public in my unmarried, pregnant state because someone from my district might see me,* she thought sadly. *I'm such a disappointment to them and my parents don't even know everything I've done since Justin died.*

"You caught on quickly. Without our *kinner* working here, we needed to hire someone. I'm thankful you wanted the job."

"*Ya*, it gets busy here."

"We need to replace inventory. I'm going to get cups of *kaffi* for Roman and me while we go over our purchase order. If you need help, let me know."

"You should take a couple of cinnamon rolls with you before I eat all of them." Isabella loved breathing in the cinnamon smell. She thought it was a *gut* marketing idea to have freshly baked breakfast items to go with the free *kaffi*. Katie sometimes made coffee cakes and all the breakfast items sold fast. Customers liked buying groceries and getting a free cup of *kaffi*. Though, there was a blue canning jar by the coffeepot if a customer wanted to donate.

"It helps out a lot that you bake the rolls and muffins in the morning."

Jenna dropped her off early at the store before she went to the hospital. On days, that Jenna didn't work, she drove the buggy to the store. Eli hitched the horse for her, so she didn't have to do it.

"I can't believe you're at the beginning of your last trimester. If you ever get tired, you can go to our office to put your feet up and take a nap. When I was pregnant with Seth, I was exhausted a lot."

"You also had two little ones to take care of when you were pregnant."

"*Ya*, it was a surprise when that happened. I suppose in some ways it was better that Lindsay kept Phoebe to raise, but I wanted all three babies."

"It seems like it all worked out with Phoebe and Seth falling in love."

Katie frowned. "I love Phoebe, but I wish she could've joined our church so that Seth wouldn't be English. I better get moving here. Roman will wonder why I'm taking so long. If you need help, just holler."

After Katie poured two cups of the steaming coffee and left to do paperwork, Isabella felt important to be left in charge of the store. Although she'd loved Justin with her whole heart, that had not been the only reason she wanted to marry him. Getting away from her abusive father had been an incentive to marry young.

Glancing around at all the wonderful items for sale gave her a sense of pride that she worked in such a place. As she restacked the puzzles on a nearby shelf, she sighed. Okay, she shouldn't feel pride and that was wrong. Amish were taught early on not to feel pride about their accomplishments. Her parents and bishop wouldn't like it either that she owned a cell phone, but she only used it for calls when necessary. She never got on the internet because knew that would bring in all kinds of worldly influences.

Although it'd been an established business when Roman bought it from his aunt, they had managed to add things to the store, like the birdhouses and quilts. She could understand why tourists liked visiting the store to find new treasures to buy. Her community liked selling their homemade soaps, produce, eggs, honey, baskets, and other things to tourists, but never in a store. They put signs at the end of their driveway to advertise what was for sale. They never put ads in the newspaper but kept their advertising simple.

I wish I could support myself and keep my baby, but the money I earn from working would not be enough. God pointed me to Eli and Jenna to be the parents. I'm thankful they want to adopt my baby.

At the sound of footsteps, she looked and saw Noah Hilty. He was tall with dark brown hair and hazel eyes. She'd noticed his eyes yesterday when he came into the store. She also knew him from the time Jenna and Eli had the church meeting at their house. It'd been right after she'd moved in with them. They had a nice conversation after church. Quickly, she stepped back to stand behind the counter, hoping he wouldn't notice her pregnancy. With only two months left, people might realize she was expecting. Even if Noah suspected she was pregnant, he wouldn't bring it up because the Amish didn't talk about having babies. It was supposed to be kept private.

"Hi." He cleared his throat. "Is Katie and Roman here today?"

"*Ya*, I can get them for you." He looked handsome in his blue shirt and dark pants.

He shook his head. "*Nee*, I'm here to ask if you'll be free to eat lunch with me."

When Lynne entered the store again, Isabella said, "I should wait on a customer. She was here earlier, and she might be back to buy a quilt."

"I can wait."

She twisted a *kapp* ribbon around her finger. "Well, I brought my lunch."

He grinned. "It doesn't have to be lunch. We can go for coffee or tea."

Out of the corner of her eye, she saw Lynne snapping a photo of the quilt with her smartphone. Would it be so terrible to have lunch with Noah? She could eat her egg salad sandwich later. But no, she shouldn't. What if someone from her church district saw her in the restaurant and told her parents? They thought she still lived with Lindsay and Harris. She needed to be able to go home after the birth of her baby. "I don't know if I should."

Katie appeared by them. "Hi, Noah."

"I was hoping Isabella would have an early lunch with me or coffee?"

Before Katie said a word, Lynne walked over to them. "I still want to buy the quilt, but my husband is fishing with his dad, so I thought I'd text a picture to him."

"Sorry I didn't put a sold sticker on it yet."

"I'll put the sticker on and take care of the customers who just walked in," Katie said, nudging her. "You should get out in the fresh air. It's such a pretty day out."

"Okay." She smiled at Noah. "I guess I'm free." What restaurant would he suggest going to? Or would he ask her opinion?

As they walked outside, Noah said, "Since it's a little early, we'll miss the lunch crowd. We can go anywhere you'd like. I have my buggy hitched out front, but we can walk too."

"I'd like to walk." *What am I thinking? If we go in the buggy, Noah might be too busy with driving to talk and ask me questions. And I've never walked in town to avoid seeing people from my church district.*

"There's a newer restaurant nearby that Eli said has good food. It's called Tilly's Diner. We can go there. How does that sound to you?"

Did Noah ask Eli where he could take me? I don't remember Eli ever speaking about Noah except once about a barn raising and what a hard worker he was. I'm overthinking this, and I doubt Noah asked Eli about me. Walking so close to him makes my heart beat faster. "Sounds good."

"I've missed you at our Sunday church meetings."

She hadn't gone with Jenna and Eli in recent weeks because she was afraid of raising questions from the church members. She'd enjoyed the prayer and Scripture readings Eli and Jenna did in their home during the week and on the off Sundays. Old Order Amish were the same as her district with church meetings every other Sunday. She gave a nervous laugh. "Is that why you came to see me today?"

Noah nodded. "Jenna and Eli told me you worked here. I'm glad you decided to go with me. I hate to eat alone."

She wondered why he didn't eat with his family. When in front of the restaurant, Isabella asked, "Don't you live with your family?"

"No, my parents retired to Sarasota a year ago. I bought their farm." He grinned. "I got it for a cheap price. I'm an only child."

"Have you gone there to visit them? I heard it's a great place to go." She bumped into him as she tried to walk faster. Her heart fluttered causing a spark to ignite in her chest. *I shouldn't feel this spark when Justin has only been gone for seven months. Maybe my pregnancy hormones make me feel emotional.*

"Sorry. I'm walking too fast."

"You're tall so it's not your fault." She took a breath. "So have you been able to go to Florida?"

"I went this winter to see *Mamm* and *Daed* and stayed a couple of weeks. It was awesome being some place warm during our cold time. They plan to come this summer to see me."

That's sad he doesn't have siblings and his parents aren't around, Isabella thought. *Of course, my parents sent me away.* After entering the diner, she noticed a sign that said to go ahead and take a seat. Glancing around at the tables and booths, relief shot through Isabella that there were no Swartzentruber Amish in her eyesight. Her family never ate at a restaurant and Rebecca's family never had when they lived here, but she thought it could happen. Tom King had no problem eating in restaurants or using take-out. She saw an empty booth. Pointing to it, she said, "Let's sit there."

Soon a waitress stood by them and handed them menus. "What would you like to drink?"

"I'd like water."

"Would you like lemon with your water?"

She shook her head. "No, thank you."

"I'll take coffee," Noah said.

"I'll be right back with your drinks."

As Isabella studied the menu, she decided on the grilled cheese sandwich with a side salad. "I know what I want."

He said, "I'm going to get the big breakfast. I only had coffee and cereal this morning."

"I imagine that was early too. Do you have livestock to take care of?"

"*Ya*, I milked the cows and fed the chickens. I finished planting the last field."

"You need more to eat after doing all that." Crazy but she wished he was sitting next to her on the same side of the booth. Though, that might be uncomfortable with her sitting close to him.

After they got their drinks, the waitress took their order. When she left, Noah smiled, showing a small dimple on his cheek. "Jenna said you've been a big help around the house. You're a woman of many talents with working at the store too."

She laughed. "Maybe I'm not. Katie seemed anxious for me to leave."

He shrugged his broad shoulders. "What can I say? Katie knows I live alone and felt sorry for me. It'd be nice to have siblings."

She disliked having to mention her family because he might ask why she lived with Jenna and Eli. It seemed the appropriate time, though, to talk about her siblings. "I have three siblings. My brother's married and I have two younger sisters."

As another waitress brought their food to the table, Noah and Isabella both murmured, "*Danki.*"

Noah said, holding a piece of toast, "*Gut,* the bread is already buttered. Some places don't butter the toast."

"Do you eat out a lot?" She took a bite of her sandwich. The cheese oozed out of her sandwich, so she wiped her mouth with a napkin.

"Probably more than I should. Katie invited me to supper a few times." He frowned. "I think she had an ulterior motive. She mentioned that Amy should go with me to a singing. Right away, Amy said that she was too old to go to singings. Or she didn't want to go with me."

"I'm sure it wasn't because she didn't want to go with you. How old are you?"

"I turned twenty-one last week." Noah took another bite of his sausage. "The food's delicious. We'll have to come here again."

She couldn't blurt out that wouldn't be possible if she lived at home again. He was Old Order Amish, so her *daed* would never allow her to date Noah. Why was she even thinking of dating Noah? Her life was complicated.

While they continued eating, Isabella steered their conversation to Noah's farm and what he planted. *That should be a safe topic to discuss,* Isabella thought. It was nice to hear Noah talk about his farm and lunchtime went by quickly.

After Noah paid the bill, they were on their way back to the store. She lost her balance as they walked on the sidewalk. He caught her before she fell to the concrete, and said, "Isabella, I got you."

An unexpected warmth surged through Isabella from his arm holding her and hearing him saying her name.

Once she was back in the store and Noah had left, hope gurgled inside her. Maybe she could fall in love again some-day. She liked Noah. Only one problem.

She was pregnant.

After Katie finished ringing up a customer's purchase of pot holders, she asked, "How was lunch?"

"It was *appeditlich*." Isabella waited until no one was near them before whispering, "Why would Noah ask me out? Doesn't he know that I'm pregnant?"

"I don't know if he does. For as far along as you are, you aren't showing much. Jenna never told him you were preg-nant. She explained you two became friends after the acci-dent. You moved in with them because things were rough at home." Katie teased, "You might be the reason he wasn't interested in Amy."

She rolled her eyes. "Or it might be because Amy wasn't. I like Noah but I shouldn't."

"Just see where it goes. His parents hated to leave Noah alone, but it was for health reasons. His *daed's* arthritis is bet-ter in the warmer weather."

When Miriam came into the store, Kate said, "I'll tell her that Lynne might buy her quilt. She'll be thrilled."

Was it possible that Noah didn't know she was pregnant? When Jenna and Eli suddenly had a baby, he would figure it out. Right now, she needed to concentrate on having a healthy baby. *I need to have an excuse ready when Noah asks me out again. I hate to hurt his feelings, but it's better not to date him. Nothing good can come from it.*

Chapter Twenty-Seven

After hitching Homer to the post, Jenna opened the door to her parents' store to get Isabella. She didn't mind picking up Isabella when necessary because she got to see her parents. Eli had taken the other buggy, so he could go directly from work to his parents to help his father with farm chores. Some days she still couldn't imagine how much her life had changed during the last few years. Leaving the place, they had grown up in Shipshewana had been difficult, but only great things had occurred because of the move. Amy and she were allowed to become EMTs. She fell in love with Eli and never would've met him if they had remained in Shipshewana.

Her life had become richer when she'd learned she had birth parents. As happy as she was for them to have baby William, Jenna wished she had a baby to love. Although Isabella wanted them to adopt her baby, her parents could intervene and change her mind. Or she could decide to keep her baby and get married. First, Tom King had been interested in the beautiful Isabella. Then after a church meeting at their house, Noah Hilty's eyes kept lingering on Isabella. He finally overcame his shyness and talked to her for several minutes.

Jenna looked around and saw her *daed* talking to a customer. He fit in so well being a store owner with his friendliness. She chuckled when she saw Isabella getting a bag from under the bakery area. *I know she saved cinnamon rolls for us. She manages to do things for us constantly.*

"Hi, Jenna. Do you have time for a cup of *kaffi*?"

She turned her head and saw her *mamm* behind her. Her mother's dark green dress and apron looked nice, but she noticed a few more gray strands of hair. It was strange how she and Amy never guessed they were adopted while growing up. Of course, Amy would say it was due to not having science, especially genetics in school. They were the only ones with black hair and brown eyes in the Yoder family and the Gingerich side. "That sounds *gut*."

As they walked to the coffee pot, Isabella looked guilty. "I did ask if I could take the rolls. I'll make fresh ones tomorrow morning."

Katie laughed. "I didn't come to stop you. I remember you asked. I'm glad you want them. We'll be closing in a couple of hours anyhow." She removed two mugs from the shelf instead of using the disposable ones. "Would you like to join us? We're taking a *kaffi* break. Roman can handle the customers during our break."

Isabella shook her head. "Abigail left a phone message earlier asking if she can stop by this evening. *Mamm* wrote a letter to me and asked Abigail to mail it for her. Of course, there isn't any point in mailing it to me when I'm not at Lindsay's house. She'll be at the phone shanty at three-thirty waiting for my call."

"Sure, tell Abigail tonight is fine," Jenna said.

"I'll go outside to call. It's such a nice day out. I won't be long."

Jenna grabbed an oatmeal cookie to eat and followed her mother to the back of the store. Once inside the office, Katie shut the door. She set her mug on the desk before pulling out a chair for Jenna. Katie sat, too, and said, "I want you to hear this from me. Isabella had lunch today with Noah Hilty. He asked her out, but she hesitated. I encouraged her to go."

"I see you decided to play matchmaker. It's okay. I could tell Noah was interested in Isabella at the church meeting. Isabella wants to do the adoption papers soon, but I hope if she gets married someday that she won't decide to ask for the baby back. I don't want us to bond and love the baby only to have him or her taken away."

"I'm sorry but I don't think Isabella will do that to you and Eli. You need to talk to her about it before you sign any papers. I want you to be able to adopt her baby, but I don't want you to be stressed wondering what she'll do later. But I don't see Isabella rushing into marriage."

"Especially to Noah. If she wants to remain in her church district and live with her parents, she can't marry him." Jenna sipped her coffee and thought, *Why are we even talking about Noah? I'm glad he got the courage to ask her out.* "There is another issue. If Isabella's parents don't allow her to live with them, where does she go? I have no problem with her staying with us for a few weeks after the birth, but I don't think it'll be the best situation. She'll get too attached to the baby. It'll be too hard for her to go ahead with the adoption."

Katie frowned. "I don't like saying this, because I love you and want the best for you and Eli, but Isabella should let Rebecca and Abe know about her pregnancy. She was close enough to them to plan to live at their house instead of with her parents. They might encourage her and the baby to move to Lancaster to live with them."

"I've told her to contact them. She hates to tell them what she and Justin did. According to Isabella, Rebecca thought Justin was perfect."

"They might not like it at first, but when they absorb the fact that the baby is a part of Justin, they will feel blessed to have his child living with them."

She exhaled a troubling breath, knowing if Isabella contacted the grandparents, she might not have a baby to adopt. It was the right thing to do though. "I agree. I'll talk to her again."

~

Isabella stared at Abigail as she put the letter from their mother on the kitchen table. Her mother wrote her about how Daniel and Ida should be settled in their house soon. They planned to get the baby in July. "I can't believe that Daniel and Ida still think they can swoop in and take my newborn. I don't want them to be my baby's parents. I'm glad you brought me *Mamm's* letter instead of mailing it to Lindsay."

"It was hard getting the buggy but fortunately, there is a volleyball game tonight. I can't stay long so I can go to it."

"It's *gut* Molly is too young to go to it and she stayed home. I hope she never finds out about my pregnancy." Isabella rubbed her forehead. "I don't know what to do. Should I tell *Mamm* now that I don't want them to adopt my baby? It doesn't seem right to give them false hope."

"I'd wait another month," Jenna said. "That way they'll still have a couple of months' notice."

Standing, Abigail said, "I better go. The youth get-together is a little distance from here." She hugged Isabella. "I can't wait until you're living at home. I miss you."

Isabella hugged her sister back. "I miss you too. I hope I can go home."

"Have fun tonight," Jenna said as Abigail walked to the door.

After Abigail left, Jenna said, "There is some pizza left."

Isabella touched her belly. "I'm stuffed. I liked how you added extra toppings to it."

"Hey, I'm great at buying a frozen pizza and throwing more toppings on it." Jenna slid the pieces off the pan to put on a plate. "I doubt Eli will be hungry. His mother is a terrific cook."

"Are you feeling okay? You didn't eat much." Isabella ran hot water into the sink to wash the few dishes and pan.

Jenna shrugged, putting the covered plate in the refrigerator. "I'm fine."

"I have my appointment tomorrow with Dr. Sullivan. I like her a lot. She wants me to see the birthing rooms at the hospital soon. When I do have the baby, it should help me to get over thinking about Justin dying at a hospital. I'm glad I'll have the baby there in a birthing room in the hospital." She stopped cleaning a plate. "Many Amish women give birth at home, but that won't happen now."

"I can take you tomorrow to your appointment. I'm off work. If you want, we can get lunch afterward." She grinned at Isabella, standing next to her to dry the plates. "I heard you enjoyed lunch today."

She laughed. "I guess Katie told you. I was a little fearful someone would see me in Tilly's Diner and tell my parents. I hate keeping the truth from them. I guess they'll know soon when I give the baby to you."

Jenna nodded. "I wish they were more understanding. I think Rebecca and Abe will be if you tell them you're pregnant."

"Okay, I'll write a letter." Isabella bit her lower lip. "Being pregnant would be a happy time if Justin hadn't died. If I keep busy, it helps me not to feel as much stress. I'm glad I have a job at the store except I worry if someone from my district will see me there."

If Isabella writes a letter soon, and Rebecca doesn't offer to have her live with them, then we can do the adoption papers.

⁓

The next day Isabella sat at a desk on the first floor. She wanted to write a letter to Rebecca before she left for her appointment. She could mail it out at the post office in town.

Dear Rebecca,

I hope you are enjoying living in Lancaster. I miss you and Abe. I asked Abigail to get your address from Tom King. I'm no longer living at home. My parents think I am living in Columbus, and I did for a short time. I'm now living with an Amish couple, Jenna and Eli. Jenna was one of the EMTs at the time of the buggy accident.

There was something I tried to tell you twice before you moved. The first time was when you told me how you and Abe had sold your house. I couldn't tell you then because I knew it would upset you what Justin and I did. When I went another time to tell you, many people were there helping you move. I am pregnant with Justin's baby. I know this will be a shock to you and Abe. I'm truly sorry but feel as grandparents you should know about our baby. My parents don't know I am writing to you. Justin and I slipped up once and decided not to tell anyone because we were going to be married. I was afraid to tell my father before the wedding. Justin mentioned telling the bishop on the night we had the buggy accident. The baby is due in July.

I waited until after Christmas to break the news to my parents. They have a couple who want to adopt my baby. After the baby is born, I will return home. They had wanted me to live with someone in Michigan. She had been a friend to my grandmother. I mentioned living with Jenna and her husband Eli. When the Michigan woman decided not to have me move in with her, my parents thought it was better to live with an English couple far enough away from Millersburg to keep my pregnancy a secret. Also, Jenna and Eli are Old

*Order Amish, so another reason my parents didn't want me to
live with them.*

*I lived with Lindsay and Harris Manning in Columbus
for a short time. They are Jenna's English parents. She and
one sister were adopted by Katie and Roman Yoder. The other
sister was raised by Lindsay. I decided to leave Harris and
Lindsay's house because their baby was going to be born in
April. They needed to have time without me living with them.
I know this is confusing, but Harris didn't know Lindsay
was pregnant with triplets. He didn't learn about them until
years later when Lindsay was diagnosed with cancer.*

Jenna came into the room. "I'll get the buggy ready for
your appointment."

"I need a few minutes to finish my letter to Rebecca."
She smiled at Jenna, wearing a raspberry-colored dress.
"You look pretty in that color. Maybe I should change out
of my drab dress."

Jenna shook her head. "You look radiant and beautiful.
Pregnancy agrees with you. I hope you have gained weight,
though. It seems like you should be showing a bigger baby
bump."

"I remember my mother didn't show much until later
with Molly. She's petite like me so you'd think we both
would show earlier."

"I'm glad you're writing to Rebecca. Take time to finish
it. We don't have to leave yet."

After Jenna left the room, she took a deep breath before
writing again.

*I don't want the Swartzentruber Amish couple to adopt
my baby. I wish I could keep my baby but don't see how that
is possible. Jenna and Eli will be great adoptive parents. My
parents don't know this yet. I like the Old Order Amish and
want the baby to have fewer restrictions and grow up in this
less conservative Amish home. Even though my parents don't*

like the Old Order Amish, I hope I can still live with them until I have enough money to move out of their house.

Please don't share this with anyone back in Millersburg. My parents don't want anyone in our district to know I'm pregnant. I've been able to keep it a secret so far that I am living close to Millersburg. By the way, I don't know if the baby is a boy or a girl. I could know from an ultrasound, but I don't what to know. It's not because I want to be surprised. Knowing if it is a son or a daughter ahead of the birth would make me feel too sad that Justin isn't here.

My address is on the envelope if you want to write me. I hope you will forgive me for not telling you earlier. I miss you all. Maybe I could visit you in the future and even look for a job in Lancaster.

Love,
Isabella

Chapter Twenty-Eight

As she sat outside under a tree, Isabella heard the birds chirping. After another night of no sleep, she decided to waddle outside to the backyard to watch the sunrise. She stared at the colorful red and pink impatiens in several flower beds. She'd helped Jenna plant the flowers. Her mother never planted flowers unless she had this spring. It was doubtful because her father would say that it was a waste of money to buy flowers for the yard. Her *mamm* liked to work in her vegetable garden, so that was acceptable to him. She provided much-needed food for the family. She'd enjoyed helping her *mamm* with canning the vegetables for winter.

Isabella had propped a pillow behind her back for comfort. Or what comfort she could try for with being so huge. The iron chair had a green floral cushion on the seat. For the last several weeks, she dozed off whenever she could. With back pain, Braxton Hicks contractions, heartburn, and an active baby in her womb, she hoped he or she came soon. What if she went past her due date? *Hopefully, that won't happen.*

She missed her job but with only a few weeks left of her pregnancy, she couldn't wait on customers. Being self-conscious of her appearance and exhaustion, Katie and Roman had understood she needed to take time off from the store. They hired another Amish woman to take her place, and Amy worked whenever she was available. June was a busy month with more tourists going through their town.

After Isabella had signed the adoption papers, she'd called her parents to tell them her decision and asked them to notify Daniel and Ida Troyer. Her father had threatened her that there would not be a home for her to return to if she disobeyed their wishes.

Sadness permeated through her that she couldn't go home after the adoption. She would be homeless. She couldn't expect to stay forever with Jenna and Eli. It'd be hard and awkward. She'd want to hold her baby but would feel like she shouldn't. She wouldn't be the mother. Jenna would be.

A couple of weeks ago, Rebecca had called her. She'd gotten her cell phone number from Hannah. Rebecca had apologized that there wasn't room for her and the baby at her in-law's house. Justin's brother and two sisters occupied two bedrooms and the third was for Rebecca and Abe. Of course, Abe's parents had the fourth bedroom. She'd said, "*Danki*, for contacting me. It was a surprise but a nice one. Although it should've happened after marriage, a baby is a blessing. I'll visit in early fall if it's okay with the adoptive parents. I want to see my first grandchild."

"I'm sure it'll be fine. Jenna and Eli are great."

"It's over six hours by car to go to Millersburg. If Abe's feeling okay, he'll be with me. I wish you would've liked Tom King. I think things could've worked out with him. If you'd told me earlier about your condition, I could've helped with getting Tom to marry you. He was crazy about you."

"I couldn't move on when my heart was broken at losing Justin."

"I know you and Justin loved each other a lot, but he wouldn't want you to grieve forever. It's sad that Justin won't be here to be a father. He would've loved having a child."

Isabella answered, "*Ya,* it is sad. It's been difficult and stressful not being able to share everything with him."

After the phone call ended, she realized that maybe it was better she and the baby couldn't live with Rebecca and Abe. Although she hadn't come out and asked if she and her baby could move in with them, she thought it could be an option. What could she tell their Amish church members? She couldn't lie and say she was a widow.

As she gazed at the beautiful pink sunrise, Isabella remembered how God loved her and He was in charge. Everything would work out according to his plan. Tiredness overtook her and soon her head dropped to a shoulder. Finally, she slept deeper than she had in many nights. She dreamed about Justin and her being together. Running her fingers over his brow, she saw how his brown eyes were full of warmth and tenderness. He held her close to his chest, whispering how much he loved her. In his embrace, she'd felt safe and glad they'd be married soon.

Jerking her head at a noise, Isabella slowly opened her eyes to see what had woken her up. She hated that her dream had been interrupted. She saw Jenna smiling at her.

"Sorry I woke you, but you looked so uncomfortable. I was afraid you'd get a sore neck."

Yawning, she still could see her beloved Justin. "I had a *wunderbaar* dream about Justin. It's too bad my dream wasn't real," her voice quivered. "It's getting warm out here."

"Do you feel like eating breakfast? I'll fix you some scrambled eggs."

"Did you already eat?"

"*Ya,* it's nine o'clock."

She rubbed her neck. "I came out to watch the sunrise. I can't believe I was outside that long. Scrambled eggs sound great."

"I'm glad you got some rest." Jenna extended her hand to Isabella to help her out of the chair. "Do you still have pelvic pain?"

She nodded, seeing concern etched in the lines on Jenna's face. "*Danki*, for taking such *gut* care of me. You and Eli have been blessings. I don't know what I would've done without you two."

~

As Isabella finished her breakfast, Jenna said, "We have our church meeting tomorrow. It's at Noah's house. His parents came to visit and help him to get ready for it. His mother cleaned the house, but I'm sure it wasn't dirty from one person living there. Noah and his dad spruced up the outside."

"I'm glad his parents came." Isabella released a deep sigh. "I miss going to the church meetings, but I'm not going tomorrow."

"I know you aren't, but I want to tell you something." *I might as well not beat around the bush, and I need to tell Isabella about Noah's questions.* Jenna pulled a chair out and sat close to Isabella. "When Noah hadn't seen you working in the store, he'd asked my *mamm* about you. She told him you'd stopped working because of health issues. Then he asked Eli and me recently if you were feeling better. I told him that it had to be kept a secret but you're pregnant. I'm sorry."

"It's okay. I shouldn't have gone out with him for lunch. I didn't tell him because it would've been embarrassing for both of us. It's *gut* you told him." Her blue eyes widened. "Was he upset to learn about my condition?"

"I don't think he was upset, but he seemed surprised. He's disappointed that you won't feel up to meeting his parents." Jenna patted her arm. "It's nice you went out with Noah. You're the first woman he's shown any interest in. That I know of. You might want to marry him someday.

Your baby would have a father and Noah's a *wunderbaar* man."

Isabella shook her head. "*Nee*, I won't change my mind about the adoption. I want you to be the mother to my baby. Even if I get married, it won't be for a long time. I feel like I'll be in limbo for some time." She smiled at Jenna. "Remember, I signed the adoption papers. You can't back out now."

"I won't change my mind. I want to make sure you're happy about everything. I did put in that I want to quit working for several months. I might not even return to work, so I can be a full-time mother. EMTs can't go part-time." Jenna smiled. "I have some other news for you. *Mamm* and *Daed* want you to live with them whenever you feel like it. There's no rush and you can stay here as long as you want after the baby's born."

"I'd like to live with Katie and Roman. That's sweet of them." She paused for a moment. "I should go home first and see if I can smooth things out with my family. The problem is I won't be able to work. As you know, I loved working at the store."

"I hope it goes okay when you return home." *I don't see her parents welcoming her with open arms,* Jenna thought.

Isabella ran her fingers through her blonde hair. "I need to brush my hair and get it pinned up and covered."

"It doesn't matter. I'm the only one here."

She responded with a girlish giggle. "I better get out of my pajamas and get dressed first before I worry about my hair."

It felt nice to hear Isabella giggle like a young girl because she was only eighteen years old. She'd been through so much with losing her fiancé and her family. "You can use the downstairs bathroom. I'll get your clothes from your bedroom."

Isabella, standing, said, "I can go upstairs. I need the exercise."

After she left the kitchen, Jenna went to her bedroom to look through the baby items she'd collected. She had a supply of cloth diapers, baby blankets, a few tiny undershirts, and short-sleeve body shirts. As she ran her fingers over the smooth maple wood of the cradle, she knew the baby would sleep in their bedroom for the first several months. Although it was nice to have a first-floor master bedroom, she wouldn't put the newborn upstairs until much later. Maybe they could make another room on the first floor into a nursery.

Amy and Phoebe wanted to have a shower for her after the baby was born. It was *gut* to wait to see if the baby was a boy or a girl. She hadn't mentioned to Isabella that they had names in mind for their baby.

Their child. It made her heart leap with joy to think they would soon be parents.

Jenna kneeled by the side of her bed to pray. "Dear Father, I give thanks to You that Isabella still wants me and Eli to adopt her precious baby. Please be with Isabella and her unborn child before birth and as she delivers. Help her parents and siblings to understand why she decided to give us her newborn. Guide them with understanding to allow Isabella to move back to their home if that is the best for her and everyone. Thank You for all your blessings. In Christ's Name, I pray, Amen."

As she stood up, Isabella's panicked voice reached her ears. "Jenna, I need your help. I'm in the bathroom."

She quickly took the stairs and opened the door. "My water broke. Do you think my labor is going to start?"

"Maybe. I'll call Dr. Sullivan." Jenna grabbed a towel to wipe up the water.

"Tell her I'm having a lot of back pain. It started last night but quit for a bit. I guess that's why I finally slept."

"It sounds like your labor started. Pain in your lower back begins during labor. It's caused by the baby's head pressing against your spine and tailbone."

"I didn't realize labor could start with back pain. I'm going to take my shower while you call the doctor. I should have time. I'm not having contractions yet."

"Okay. I'll be back soon." As Jenna hurried to call, she decided to use her cell phone instead of going to the barn to use their landline.

She sat down in the living room to call. *I'm not the one in labor, but I feel nervous and excited. I'll soon have a baby to love. And I have felt a part of Isabella's pregnancy. Many times, I've felt the baby kick in the womb. Isabella hadn't been shy and wanted me to feel the baby's movement.*

At nine o'clock that night, Isabella gave birth to a girl weighing six pounds and eight ounces. Jenna had stayed with her during the long labor except for a brief time to get something to eat. Isabella looked exhausted but relieved to have it over with as she held her tiny baby. "She's beautiful, isn't she?"

Jenna nodded. "*Ya,* she is beautiful."

"*Danki* for staying with me. Your support during the long labor helped me a lot."

"You did great. I'm proud of you."

Isabella kissed the baby and gazed at her for a long moment. Then smiling at Jenna, she said, "It's your turn to hold her."

As Jenna took the baby into her arms, she said, "She's so precious. Such a miracle from God."

"She is. God got me through the labor. I couldn't believe when we got here, I was only dilated two fingers." Isabella sipped her apple juice from a straw. "I'm tired but a *gut* kind of tired."

Jenna thought about how happy Eli had looked to see the baby. He'd left to call Isabella's family and Hannah. He planned to give the birth news to their parents too. He'd have Lindsay call Phoebe and Seth because he didn't want to be away any longer than necessary from his daughter.

"The nurse should be back soon with something for you to eat."

"Do you and Eli have a name picked out for her?" Isabella asked.

"I like the name, Rachel."

"That's a *wunderbaar* name."

"So, her full name will be Rachel Isabella Zimmerman."

Tears filled Isabella's blue eyes. "I love she'll have my name too."

Chapter Twenty-Nine

Five months later

Jenna didn't care she hadn't gotten pregnant as many women did after adopting a baby. Whenever God blessed her with another baby, it'd be fine with her. For now, she was happy to be a mother to Rachel. When the time was right, she'd be told about her birth parents. Jenna didn't want Rachel's adoption to be kept secret for years.

At the sound of a knock, she went to the kitchen door. When she saw Isabella, Jenna said, "You don't have to knock. You're family."

Isabella laughed. "I think everyone is family to you."

"I do seem to have a lot of family." Jenna opened the oven door to check on her pies. "They aren't quite done. I'm baking them for Thanksgiving."

"I could've baked pies for you." Isabella removed her coat and draped it over a chair. She wore a lavender dress and a matching apron. "I'm still bringing a green bean casserole."

"That's *gut*. Would you like a cup of coffee? Rachel's taking a morning nap."

"Coffee would be great. I'm chilled from riding in the buggy, even though it isn't that cold yet." She untied her black bonnet that was over her *kapp* and placed it with her coat. "I have news to share. Well, I guess I can wait until Noah comes inside. He's in the barn talking to Eli."

As Jenna poured the coffee into mugs, Isabella continued, "Never mind. I can't wait. Noah and I are getting married the last Thursday in January."

She set the mugs on the table and hugged Isabella. "Congratulations." Although Jenna knew Isabella had recently started to go with Noah to singings, she was surprised.

"I was going to wait longer, but it's been over a year now since…Justin died." Isabella frowned, taking a breath. "We'll get married at Noah's house. Obviously, I can't have it at my parents' place since they kicked me out."

There was no reason to mention it wasn't possible to get married in her family's church district. She was marrying out of their Swartzentruber Amish faith. Jenna pulled out a chair to sit across from Isabella. "It's a shame you only got to stay two months."

"It probably didn't help that I wanted to go back to work at the store. When I heard that the woman they'd hired to take my place had quit, I wanted to work for Katie and Roman again. And I couldn't see Noah while I lived at home. I couldn't stand not seeing him. It's ridiculous because Noah is Amish too."

A blast of cold air came in with Noah as he entered the kitchen. Eli was close behind him. Noah looked at Isabella and laughed. "I knew you couldn't wait until I came in to share our wedding news."

Isabella shook her head. "Geez, you have such great hearing. I'll have to remember that."

"I could tell you spilled our news from your beaming face."

After they removed their black hats and coats, Eli nudged Noah. "Hey, you know better. Women love to talk about weddings. I'm guessing this means you two are getting hitched."

"*Ya*, Isabella's agreed to be my *fraa*." Noah grinned. "It's a *gut* thing because I didn't want to ride the bus by myself to go to Sarasota this winter."

Eli put their hats and coats on hooks by the door.

Isabella, smiling, said, "That's another reason why I said we should get married in January. I want to see the ocean. It'll be nice to be in Florida for a honeymoon."

"We should celebrate this happy news. I'll get cookies out of the jar, but first I should get my pies out of the oven."

"I'll pour their coffee," Isabella said as she went to get cups out of the cabinet. "Katie's going to sew my wedding dress. Noah's mother insists she wants to sew his suit."

As she grabbed potholders to get her pies out of the oven, Jenna tried to think if she'd have enough time to make a quilt for Isabella and Eli. She could get help from her *mamm* and Amy, but it'd be hard to keep it a secret since Isabella lived with them. She should ask Colleen to help with the quilting. *I imagine my mamm is thrilled at her matchmaking skills. Now if we can only find someone for Amy.*

She put the pies on the cooling racks and turned to look at Isabella. "You'll love seeing the ocean. When Mom took us on a cruise, I couldn't believe how blue the water was. It was special sharing it with my mom and sisters."

"I'm glad you had this experience. I can't *wait* to see the ocean."

Noah put his hand on his chest. "What about you can't *wait* to marry me?"

She rolled her eyes at him. "That too."

"You'll be a beautiful bride. You haven't met Noah's parents yet. Are they coming for Christmas?" Jenna thought, *wouldn't the parents of an only child want to meet their future daughter-in-law before the wedding?*

Noah sipped his coffee. "They plan to come around the middle of January."

"We've talked on the phone." Isabella took a plate of oatmeal and chocolate chip cookies to the table.

Noah and Isabella talked about whom they should ask to be their wedding attendants. Isabella knew she would like Abigail and Hannah to be hers, but that wasn't possible. Hannah had married Luke in the fall. Amish attendants couldn't be married. After they wiped out all the cookies on the plate, Noah and Isabella said they had errands to get done. Isabella rinsed out their mugs and said, "We better go."

Noah helped her with her coat, then he got his. "We'll see you tomorrow."

Isabella hugged Jenna. "*Danki* for the cookies. Bye."

After the couple left, Jenna laughed, looking at the empty plate. "Do you suppose they had skipped breakfast?"

"I had to quickly grab two cookies because I've seen how much Noah eats." Eli took her hand in his. "Your cookies are the best, though. No one can resist them."

"Do you think Isabella wants to hurry to get married to have a baby? It doesn't seem like going to Florida would be the only reason they want to have their wedding so soon."

Eli shrugged. "I think they're excited to be in love and want to be together. Noah's a farmer so January's a great time for him to get married."

Jenna heard cute babbling sounds coming from their bedroom. "Rachel's awake. She's such a *gut* baby."

"I'll get her." Eli jumped up from his chair and left the kitchen.

She whispered, "That baby has her *daed's* heart, that's for sure and certain. And she has mine."

About the Author

Diane graduated from the Ohio State University with a bachelor's degree. She met her husband, Tom, while teaching at an orphanage. They enjoy their life in Ohio and have been blessed with six children and several grandchildren.

Diane started writing nonfiction and was published in *Woman's World* and *The Catholic Telegraph*. Later, she decided it would be a nice escape to write fiction. She wanted to keep her sanity in the midst of a large family.

Two daughters, who were born with Down syndrome, live with them. Diane's favorite vacation is going to the beach with her family. She gives thanks for all her blessings, including being in remission from Non-Hodgkin's lymphoma.

Diane is the author of Amish fiction, historical Christian fiction, inspirational contemporary romance, and chick-lit mystery. She is represented by literary agent Lesley Sabga of The Seymour Agency. To connect with Diane, please visit **www.dianecraver.com** and https://www.facebook.com/Diane-Craver-153906208887/

Dear Reader

Thank you for reading *An Unexpected Gift*. I hope you enjoyed reading my book. If so, please consider leaving me a book review on Amazon, and other online places. I'd love to hear what you thought. It was wonderful to continue with the adoption theme in this book. Adoption among the Old Order Amish and New Order Amish is a long tradition in many communities.

You might wonder how it is possible for my characters, Jenna and Amy, to be Emergency Medical Technicians when they are Amish. I read in *The Budget* newspaper that the Swiss Valley Joint Ambulance District in Ohio wanted some Amish to be EMTs. Two Amish sisters, Karen and Miriam, wanted to do something in the medical field, so they took the EMT class. Then they took a standardized test to obtain certification. Both passed on their first try.

If you haven't followed me on BookBub, please sign up here: https://www.bookbub.com/profile/diane-craver. I couldn't do this job I love without your support, and I never take it for granted.

Blessings,

Coconut Cream Pie Recipe

My sweet mother, Laoma Oberly Wilson, loved to bake all kinds of pies and cookies. I decided to include one of the pies she loved to make.

Ingredients
   ¼ cup cornstarch
   ⅔ cup sugar
   ¼ teaspoon salt
   2 cups milk (scalded)
   3 egg yolks (beaten)
   2 tablespoons butter
   1 teaspoon pure vanilla extract
   ¼ cup toasted coconut
   8 oz. Cool Whip
   9-inch pre-baked pie shell

Directions

1. Combine cornstarch, sugar, and salt. Add milk and mix well.
2. Pour a small amount over beaten eggs, mix, and return to the mixture. Mix together.
3. Cook over low heat or use a double boiler until the mixture thickens. Add butter and vanilla, then add the desired amount of sweetened coconut (approx. ¼ cup) to mixture.
4. Pour the mixture into a pre-baked pie shell. Allow to cool to room temperature.
5. After the mixture cools, top the pie with 8 oz. cool whip.

6. Toast some coconut (approx. 1/3 cup) and sprinkle over the top of the pie.
7. Chill for several hours and enjoy!

Acknowledgments

Thank you to my awesome agent, Lesley Sabga, for telling me she loved my voice and for wanting me as a client. I appreciate her continued hard work on my behalf.

I give thanks to God for all my blessings as an author and for His inspiration as I write.

Thank you to my husband and children for all their continued support and love.

Thanks to the following team at Vinspire Publishing:

Dawn Carrington, for giving me this opportunity to publish my Amish stories.

Kassy Paris, for your editing expertise and your great insight about my characters and storyline. You helped me write a better story.

Elaina Lee, for designing this beautiful cover for *An Unexpected Gift*.

A huge thanks to Susan Lantz Simpson and Laurie Stroup Smith for their writing endorsements. I appreciate you both taking the time out of your busy schedules to read *An Unexpected Gift*.

Plan Your Next Escape!

What's Your Reading Pleasure?

Whether it's captivating historical romance, intriguing mysteries, young adult romance, illustrated children's books, or uplifting love stories, Vinspire Publishing has the adventure for you!

For a complete listing of books available, visit our website at www.vinspirepublishing.com.

Like us on Facebook at
www.facebook.com/VinspirePublishing

Follow us on Twitter at
www.twitter.com/vinspire2004

Follow us on Instagram at
www.instagram.com/vinspirepublishing

We are your travel guide to your next adventure.

Printed in Great Britain
by Amazon